BOOKS BY JOAB STIEGLITZ

The Utgarda Trilogy

The Old Man's Request

The Missing Medium

The Other Realm

The Thule Trilogy

The Hunter in the Shadows:

The Other Realm

Book Three of the Utgarda Series

Joab Stieglitz

In memory of Steve Russell, without whose expertise,
assistance, and encouragement this book would never have
been published.

DEDICATION

This book is dedicated to my wife, without whose continual support and relentless encouragement it may never have been finished.

ACKNOWLEDGMENTS

I would like to acknowledge all the people who inspired, encouraged, assisted, and supported me through this effort.

Many thanks to Steph, Greg, Jenna, and Josiah for wading through my drafts and proposing, or demanding, edits, changes, and other suggestions.

Thanks to the Springfield Writers group for listening, critiquing, and suggesting things that made the story all the better, especially Carol, David, Fred, and Duane.

Chapter 1

July 16, 1929

Father Sean O'Malley looked pensively out the window of the train compartment. The weather was bleak. The sky was gray, and raindrops struck the glass and slipped horizontally across its surface as the train sped past the hills and farms. He shared the compartment with anthropologist Anna Rykov, and Dr. Harold Lamb. Rykov was asleep on the bench across from the priest, while Lamb reading the newspaper.

"Still no bodies found in the wreckage of the Church of Cosmic Understanding," the doctor said, pulling O'Malley from his musings. "You think they would have found someone by now."

"Perhaps it's for the better," O'Malley said. The Church of Cosmic Understanding had been the cover organization for a cult of worshippers of Utgarda, a malevolent entity that

Rykov, Lamb, and O'Malley had been charged with banishing by their late benefactor, Jason Longborough. "The discovery of Utgarda's minions would certainly have caused a stir."

With the help of some gangsters, the three had interrupted a ritual that had attempted to bring Utgarda to Manhattan from its home dimension. In the subsequent battle, some of the cultists had been transformed into winged monsters will tentacled faces and claws.

"Never mind the cultists," Lamb said in exasperation, "what about Ganon?" Anna and Lamb had been accosted by a vagrant in the Subway who knew them by other names. Lamb later discovered that the man was, in fact, Preston Carver, his company commander during the Great War, who had lost his memory. The man believed that he was Ganon, a transplanted cavalry officer from the same place as Utgarda.

"Yes," Anna said wearily, stretching as she slowly rose into a sitting position. "Ganon was our only tangible connection between Brian Teplow's stories and Utgarda. How do we follow the trail without him?"

"Our first priority is to collect Brian from Oak Valley Sanitarium," O'Malley replied, "and return him to his mother."

Brian Teplow was a celebrity spirit medium who had disappeared mysteriously. Jason Longborough had met with Teplow shortly before the trustee's death. In searching for Teplow to learn the contents of that conversation, Anna and Lamb had uncovered Brian's childhood sketchbook. In it, were photographic-quality drawings of Anna, Lamb, Ganon, and a woman named Liv Lee on an expedition in an exotic land that Teplow had drawn ten years earlier. Subsequent investigation revealed that the realm in the drawings was the home dimension of Utgarda, and the depicted expedition was to rescue Brian from Gho-Bazh, Utgarda's rival.

"Once we have Brian," Lamb added, "he may be able to fill in some gaps as to how all of this fits together. After all, he is the common thread to this whole affair."

"How long until we reach Chatham?" Anna asked. Lamb glanced at his watch.

"Another hour-and-a-half," he replied. "Assuming we can find transportation, we should have him in our custody by five or so."

The three had left Penn Station in Manhattan on the 10:30 AM express train, which was scheduled to deposit them in the small town of Chatham, New York, around 3:45. From there, they would need to hire a car to take them to the Oak Valley Sanitarium a few miles outside of the town.

"If not," Anna said, "we will need to find accommodations for the night and catch the first train back in the morning."

◆

The storm had passed by the time the train arrived in Chatham. A thick fog rose as the wet surfaces quickly dried in the hot July sun.

"There seems to be quite a crowd on the platform," Lamb noted as the train pulled into the station. In addition to obvious travelers, the doctor noticed spectators, entertainers, and vendors among the crowd, giving their arrival an almost carnival-like atmosphere.

As the train lurched to a halt, a brass band started playing Stars and Stripes Forever and a cheer erupted from the crowd, which rose anew when the people emerged from the carriages. Lamb held out a hand for Anna while creating a space at the foot of the steps for her to step onto the platform. The crowd had closed in around the debarking passengers.

O'Malley followed behind Anna, and at the sight of the priest, the onlookers in the front stepped back as far as those pressed behind them would allow. O'Malley took the lead, and the assembly parted to allow them through. The other passengers quickly followed suit, and soon there was a line leading from the car the priest had emerged from to the station house.

Once inside Union Station, the crowd was greatly reduced, though still significant. Only people having business with one of the three railroads were permitted inside. The New York and Harlem Railroad, the Boston and Albany Railroad, and the Rutland Railroad to Vermont all converged in Chatham, and customers mobbed the ticket windows.

Lamb took the lead and forged a path through the throng to the street-side exits. Once on the street, he looked around for a taxi, but there were no vehicles of any kind in sight.

"I wonder where we can catch a cab," the doctor said loud enough to be heard by Anna and O'Malley over the noise of the crowd.

"You won't find any cars or carriages in the center of town," a smiling man in a straw hat said. "They close off the square on convergence days."

"How's that?" Lamb asked.

"Convergence days," the man said, as if it was obvious. Then he explained, "When trains from all three lines arrive around the same time." He paused, waiting for comprehension. "The station can only handle one train in each direction, so there's a big delay while the folks get off their trains and wait for the train they want. The trains all have to offload their passengers, and then come back to receive the new ones. Since there's a captive audience, the town sets up a little celebration. It's good for business and the folks don't have to just sit around waiting."

"There seems to be a lot of people here today," Anna said. "More people than can comfortably appreciate the festivities."

"Yours was the last of the three trains," the man said. "People will clear out in an hour or so now that the trains are reboarding."

"Do you know where we might find a taxi?" O'Malley asked.

"There isn't much call for taxis around here," the man replied, "but you might be able to hire a car over at the lunch counter in Woolworth's."

"Thank you, sir," Anna said with a smile. "You have been very helpful." At the sound of Anna's Russian accent, the man's demeanor soured momentarily, but he recovered quickly and tipped his hat before disappearing into the crowd.

◆

Half an hour later, Anna, Lamb, and O'Malley were seated in an Ajax Nash sedan, Anna and Lamb sat in the back. A large, black, barrel-chested mutt with a white stripe down his eyes and around his muzzle sat between them eyeing Anna suspiciously.

"Don't mind Cletus," Shane said. "He's all show. So what brings you folks out here to the sanitarium? Visiting someone?"

"We're here to bring someone home," Lamb replied. "If you don't mind, we would appreciate it if you could wait while we collect his things, and then bring us back to the station."

"We'll make it worth your while," O'Malley added. The driver glanced at the priest.

"I suppose we could wait," Shane said after a moment. "We've got no place to be this afternoon."

"How soon until we arrive?" Anna asked. As with the man at the station, the driver was taken aback by her accent. Cletus sat up straight and turned his head to watch Anna. She did not react.

"Um," the driver started, then glanced sidelong at O'Malley with concern. O'Malley gave him a quizzical look back. "It's about five miles," the driver continued. "We should be there in about twenty minutes."

"What can you tell us about the sanitarium?" Lamb asked.

"Never been inside the place," Shane replied. "Got a good reputation."

"Do you know anyone who has been a patient there?" Anna asked. The driver was still distracted by her accent. Sensing Shane's continued discomfort, Cletus growled quietly. Anna ignored it.

"Folks from around here can't afford that place," Shane replied. "Mostly people from the city from what I've heard."

"Do you know anyone who works at Oak Valley Sanitarium?" O'Malley asked.

"I knew a girl who was a maid there," the driver replied. "Don't know if she's still there, though. Her name's Delores Bulch." At the mention of the name, Cletus wagged his tail. "Maybe she can tell you something useful." He glanced back at Anna in the rear-view mirror. "Tell me why you're really here."

"We are here to collect one of the patients," Lamb replied. "He was brought here against his will."

"His mother asked us to bring him home," O'Malley added.

◆

Anna and O'Malley were at the open glass doors when a matronly woman in a nurse's uniform intercepted them and blocked their way.

"I'm sorry," the woman said with authority, "but this is a private facility." Lamb joined them.

"We are here to collect Brian Teplow," O'Malley said

"He has been confined here unwillingly," Lamb stated as he presented Mrs. Teplow's letter. "He was registered under the name Daniel Meldon." The nurse took the paper from Lamb and read it.

"We have been tasked with bringing him home," Anna added. The nurse looked up from the paper and eyed Anna suspiciously.

"Wait over there," the nurse said, pointing to a comfortable sitting area as she led the three into the building. As an afterthought, she added, "Help yourself to some lemonade," and smiled ingenuously.

Chapter 2

July 16, 1929

Anna walked over to the pitcher and poured herself a glass, gesturing to the others as she did. O'Malley nodded, and she handed him the glass before pouring another for herself.

Lamb watched the nurse walk over to the reception desk and pick up a candlestick telephone. She glanced toward the visitors several times while speaking in a low voice. When she hung up, she strode purposefully back to the three.

"Mr. Wilkinson will be here in a moment," the nurse said to Lamb with cold civility before returning to the desk.

"Thank you," Lamb replied in a similar tone, and then took a seat next to Anna.

"Something does not seem right," Anna said with suspicion.

"Indeed," O'Malley agreed. "She didn't even ask us who we were."

A moment later, a nervous-looking man in a mourning suit and pince-nez approached quickly from a side hall. He noted the three and walked to the desk. The nurse handed him Mrs. Teplow's letter. He read it, adjusted his tie, and then stepped toward Lamb with his hand out.

"Good afternoon," the man said with practiced composure, "I'm Mr. Wilkinson, the facility administrator." Lamb took his hand and shook firmly. Wilkinson blanched slightly at the grip.

"Good afternoon, sir," Lamb replied. "We're here to collect Brian Teplow, who was admitted to this hospital under false pretenses."

"And you are," Wilkinson glanced at the paper, "Dr. Harold Lamb, I take it."

"I am," Lamb replied. "And my colleagues are Dr. Anna Rykov, and Father Sean O'Malley, as mentioned in the letter." He gazed squarely at the administrator. "I trust there will be no difficulty preparing Mr. Teplow for travel."

Wilkinson smiled sheepishly, blotted some sweat from his balding head, and said, "I'm afraid Mr. Meldon, uh, Teplow, is no longer a guest of Oak Valley."

'Where is he?" Lamb asked with irritation.

"He was released into Dr. Langford's care over a week ago," Wilkinson replied. I don't know where Mr. Teplow is now," Wilkinson stammered nervously. "He didn't leave a forwarding address." An idea bloomed in his eyes. "Perhaps his guardian, Mr. Frank, knows where to find him."

"Woody Frank is dead," O'Malley said flatly. "He was murdered." Wilkinson's mouth gaped in horror.

"He had no authority to commit Brian Teplow to a sanitarium in the first place," Anna added.

"Your former patient might be in danger," Lamb said, "so it's best that we get him to the safety of his own home."

"But I already told you, I don't know where he is."

"Where might we find this Dr. Langford," Anna asked, emphasizing her accent to intimidate the administrator. Wilkinson glanced from Lamb to Anna, and then noticed O'Malley behind them peering with his most judgmental, priestly gaze.

"Dr. Martin Langford," Wilkinson said. "He has an office in town."

"Let's give him a call," Lamb said.

◆

A few minutes later, the four were seated in Wilkinson's office. The administrator put the receiver to his ear and held the base before his face.

"Hello, Agnes?" he said into the mouthpiece, "put me- yes, hello-Put- yes, it's lovely out now that the rain has passed." He arched his eyebrows at Anna, but her expression remained neutral.

"Agnes," Wilkinson said forcefully, then he added more calmly, "put me through to Dr. Langford's office in town, please." He frowned as he listened to the voice on the other end of the connection. "Oh, I see. You're sure?" He shook his head. "Very well. Yes, put me through to his house, please." He placed his hand over the mouthpiece.

"Agnes says that Dr. Langford closed his office for a couple of weeks and may be out of town," the administrator. "She's patching me through to his home now."

"Yes?" Wilkinson said at the return of the voice on the telephone. "What?" He signed heavily. "Thank you, Agnes." He put the base back on the desk, hung up the receiver, and rested his head in his hands.

"What has happened?" Anna asked with urgency.

"Dr. Langford's home phone has been disconnected," Wilkinson replied. "Agnes said that she was not aware of a suspension of service. Probably a tree fell in the storm and pulled down the wires."

"I see," Anna said. "Where does Dr. Langford live?"

"Not far from here," the administrator replied.

"I surmised that much from him having an office in town," she said curtly.

"We need to find Brian Teplow and return him to New York," Lamb glared at Wilkinson. O'Malley noted the tension in the room.

"Perhaps you could provide us with his address," the father said, "and we can pursue our inquiries with Dr. Langford." Seeing the out, the administrator relaxed slightly.

"Of course," Wilkinson said, grabbing a pencil and paper to write down the address.

"Both home and office, please," Anna said.

"With the telephone numbers," Lamb added. "And while you're at it," he added with equal abruptness, "have your staff see if they have any records of Teplow's departure. Did he call a taxi, or get a ride from someone?"

"Of course," the administrator said mechanically as he handed the paper to Anna.

"Has anyone used his room since his departure?" O'Malley asked, seeking to ease the tension again.

"No," Wilkinson replied, "I don't believe so. Summer is a slow period for us," he added conversationally. O'Malley smiled.

"Then we would like to see his room," Anna said.

"Right this way," Wilkinson said, gesturing toward the door.

◆

When they arrived at the designated room, there was a maid dusting. Wilkinson knocked on the door frame. The woman jumped at the sound.

"I'm sorry, Delores," Wilkinson said. "These people are looking for Brian Teplow, um, Daniel Meldon."

"So he really was Brian Teplow," the maid said in surprise. "Dr. Langford checked him out last week."

"Did Mr. Teplow leave anything behind?" Anna asked. The maid noted Anna's accent and looked to Wilkinson, who nodded.

"You can speak freely to them, Delores," the administrator said.

"Well, ma'am," Delores said after clearing her throat, "Brian was very tidy, and didn't have much with him other than the clothes he was wearing. It's hard to forget a grown man in night sleepers." She grinned at the memory. When she noted Anna's confusion, she added, "Pajamas with feet."

"And that is all he had with him?" O'Malley asked.

"That's all I ever saw him in," Delores replied. "His closet was empty."

"So," Lamb said in Wilkinson's face, "he was admitted to your facility, under false pretenses, with only pajamas in his possession?" Wilkinson was shaken. "Doesn't that strike you as peculiar?"

"Mr. Meldon, uh, Teplow, was brought here in the middle of the night," Wilkinson blurted out defensively. "I wasn't here at the time." He glanced at each of the three newcomers nervously. "I was told it was by special arrangement with Dr. Langford."

"And does Dr. Langford have many 'special patients'?" Anna asked skeptically.

"All his patients are special," Wilkinson replied. "He's not a regular member of the staff. He only sees a few patients here."

"And what was his interest in Mr. Teplow?" Lamb asked.

"I'm not involved in the treatment of the patients," Wilkinson continued, "and Dr. Langford is especially private about his clients."

"So you had no idea who the patient really was," O'Malley said, "why he was here, or where he went?" The father was starting to lose his composure.

"I know where he went," Delores said, averting her eyes when she caught Wilkinson's glare. Anna noticed the exchange and glared back at the administrator.

"Where did he go?" Anna asked with a smile. Delores glanced at Wilkinson and gulped.

"Dr. Langford offered Mr. Teplow the use of his guest house," the maid said. "The doctor said there were too many distractions, and that the sanitarium was not the right place to treat him."

"Is there anything else you can tell us that might help us find Brian?" O'Malley asked with urgency.

"Nothing I can think of," Delores replied, shaking her head. "He was a nice guy. I hope you find him."

"You have been very helpful, Delores," Anna said with a friendly smile. "Shane Patterson sends his regards," she added before turning to leave.

"You may be hearing from us again," Lamb said to Wilkinson. He handed the administrator a business card. "You will call this number if you have any additional information." He turned toward the door before Wilkinson could reply.

"Of course," echoed behind the three as they exited the building.

Chapter 3

July 16, 1929

"Do you know where this is?" Anna asked Shane as she sat in the front seat of the car. Cletus poked his muzzle over the seat to watch her as Anna handed the paper to the driver.

"That's a ways down the 'pike in Brume Hollow," he replied. "It might take an hour or so to get there."

"Why so long?" Lamb asked as he closed the rear door. "We were told that the resident works in town."

"Those windy roads are tough to navigate," Shane replied. "Especially when in this fog." The three had failed to notice that fog had engulfed the area while they were inside. "It'll linger in the woods for a while longer."

"Well, it's imperative that we find Mr. Teplow as soon as possible," O'Malley said. "If you would continue to assist us, it would be a truly Christian service."

"And I will donate another five dollars for your troubles," Anna added.

"Well, you folks have been good to me," Shane said without hesitation, "and this feels like an adventure in a dime novel. Count me in."

"Good man," Lamb said in approval, and patted the driver's shoulder.

Gravel sprayed behind the Nash and left divots as the car sped off down the fog-shrouded drive.

◆

As predicted, the going was slow. Shane turned in the opposite direction upon leaving the Oak Valley Sanitarium driveway. The road devolved down to a dirt track within a few miles. It wound into a dense stand of old oaks, where the little sunlight that broke through the thick, towering canopy barely pierced the blanketing fog.

As they entered the encroaching forest, Cletus' attention drifted from Anna to their surroundings, and he growled ominously, alternating between stepping across Lamb and O'Malley to peer out the windows.

"This is Brume Hollow," Shane said as he slowed around a winding curve along the bank of a defile containing a babbling brook.

"It seems like it would be quite lovely when the fog is gone," Anna said, admiring the creek as it flowed through some rocky outcroppings.

"There aren't too many people out here," the driver continued, "being that the roads are so dangerous." O'Malley sensed there was more to it.

"This seems like prime real estate," the priest said with curiosity. "Surely some industrious speculator has considered developing this area."

"The country folk won't come here," Shane replied. "They say these woods are haunted." He paused to concentrate on a sharp turn. "Some city folks have disappeared here over the years."

"That seems a little fantastic," Lamb said suspiciously.

"God's honest truth," Shane replied defensively. "There was a young couple just last spring found all chewed up. They said it looked like they'd been attacked by a bear. And then there was that fellow with the broken neck. They said he fell off a cliff. There were others come out here and were never seen again. As you can see for yourselves, if you don't know these parts and get trapped in a fog like this, the going can be treacherous."

"Indeed," Anna said introspectively. This is a very remote address for a psychiatrist, she thought. Especially one who invites patients to use his guest house. On the other hand, the seclusion might be beneficial for the treatment of certain conditions.

The car slowed to a stop at the end of the dirt road, where a pair of iron gates blocked passage beyond an ancient, eight-foot-high brick wall.

"This must be the place," O'Malley said.

"It doesn't look like anyone has been here in a while," Lamb said. The gates were locked with a rusted chain and old but serviceable padlock on the outside. Beyond the gate, an overgrown path disappeared into the trees and up a small hill.

"There must be another entrance to the estate if Dr. Langford lives here and commutes into the village," Anna said.

"I suppose so," Shane replied. "Maybe there's a driveway on the other side of the hill. But this is the road on your paper."

"No one is faulting you, Shane," O'Malley said reassuringly. "We traveled quite a distance into the forest. Given the condition of the road, Dr. Langford must have another means of egress."

"And I haven't seen any telephone poles since we left the main road from the hospital," Lamb added. "We'd best turn around and look for the driveway he uses."

"I wouldn't mind getting out of the hollow before the sun goes down," Shane said uneasily. He put the car into reverse and backed up to the side to turn around. It started backward slowly, but then the rear end dropped, and the car slipped a little, stopping abruptly with a clunk. Cletus barked.

When Shane put the car back into a forward gear, the wheels spun to no effect. Lamb leapt out, followed by Cletus. The dog circled the car, while the doctor stepped to the rear. The back of the car was completely clear of the ground, which dropped a couple of feet beyond the tall grass that had concealed it.

◆

"That's gonna need a tow truck," Shane said twenty minutes later. He, Lamb, and O'Malley had tried a variety of methods to free the car from its predicament, but the soft ground and the purchase from the gully below were insufficient to get any leverage.

"Then we need to find out if anyone is at home," Anna said, indicating the gates.

"Under ordinary circumstance," Lamb said, "I would respect the occupant's privacy. But we have no alternative. It's several miles back to the main road. The house is probably closer."

"We should all keep together," O'Malley said to Shane.

"Cletus and I will stay here," he replied, "in case somebody comes down this way. If so, I'll toot the hooter." He squeezed the ball at the end of the horn to demonstrate.

"As you wish," O'Malley replied.

"And we will pay for any damages to your vehicle," Anna added.

When Anna stepped out of the car, Cletus started barking and carefully approached her. Anna stopped and held out her hand to the dog. Cletus stepped up, sniffed the offered hand, and then hopped into the driver seat.

"We'll see if we can get a tow truck, or if Dr. Langford has a tractor or something will can pull the car up with," Lamb said. He handed Shane one of his business cards. "If you run into any difficulty, this will validate your story." He shook Shane's hand and then joined O'Malley at the gates.

The priest examined the lock more closely. Then he pulled at the chains and tested the give of the iron bars of the gate.

"This lock is newer than the chain," he said as Anna joined them. "And both are newer than the gates." He pulled at the gates, and the centermost bars started to bend. "I think we can pull these apart enough to squeeze through."

"It's worth a try," Lamb said. He took hold of the bar on one side and pulled. At the same time, O'Malley pulled on the other. Their muscles strained as the two exerted themselves, and they managed to bend the bars slightly, but the chain was not long enough to part the gates sufficiently. Then they both fell backward as the gates suddenly opened. Anna and Shane laughed as she held up the lock, which she had managed to pick with a pin and a nail file from her purse.

"That should enable us to bring a tractor back if we find one," she said with a grin.

Lamb patted down his trousers, feeling the wet, muddy stain on his rear, and scowled at Anna. She put her hand before her face to cover her grin.

"We probably should have tried that first," O'Malley said, dusting off his cassock. He had landed in dry gravel.

"Let's go," Lamb said, taking the lead through the gates. O'Malley followed. Anna turned back to nod at Shane. He acknowledged the gesture. Then she turned and hastened her pace to catch up with the others.

◆

Following the path beyond the gate led the trio up a small hill where, completely concealed from the gate, stood several old, weather-beaten, wooden structures. Their paint was chipped and faded, but all showed signs of sporadic maintenance.

The main house, a large Victorian with a wrap-around porch, sat before the overgrown, circular driveway. To one side of the house stood a detached garage that sagged slightly to one side. The twin doors hung askew. Beyond those structures, barely visible between them through the fog, was what looked like a barn and a small cottage.

All was quiet and the air was still. The sound of their footsteps through the fallen leaves seemed to thunder in the silence. The shadows of the tall trees scattered throughout as the weak sunset cast a grim pall over the estate.

"Doesn't look like anyone has been here in a while," Lamb mused, "and I don't see any signs of another exit."

"Someone has been maintaining the place," O'Malley said. "There are no broken windows, and some of the walls have been patched more recently than the underlying structures."

"Perhaps this is not the actual residence," Anna suggested. She started toward the cottage. It was a small, two-story Cape Cod with a single dormer over the front door. As it became more distinct through the fog, Anna noticed that it was in relatively good repair compared to the other buildings.

"That must be the guest house," Lamb said as he and O'Malley caught up with Anna.

"Shouldn't we try the main residence first?" O'Malley asked. "It wouldn't be proper to poke around without announcing ourselves."

"Neither house appears to be occupied," Anna said, "but that one is in better condition, which suggests more recent occupation."

As they rounded the main house so that the cottage was in full view, they could see wires suspended from poles leading into the woods behind the cottage.

"There," Lamb said with confidence, "the cottage is in use, and there must be at least a maintenance road to service those telephone lines."

"At least we should be able to call for a tow truck," O'Malley said with relief. He leapt up the three steps to the front door and knocked. "Hello? Dr. Langford? Mr. Teplow?" There was no response. "Hello? Our car is stuck on the road down below. May we use your telephone?"

When there was still no response from inside the house the priest tried the door, and it opened easily. Beyond the doorway was a foyer, with a stairway leading up along one side. To the right of the steps was a door. O'Malley stepped carefully into the foyer. The floorboards squeaked loudly in the absence of any other sound other than the ticking of a grandfather clock to the right of the door.

"Hello?" he called again. Anna and Lamb entered the foyer and the doctor quietly closed the door behind him. "There doesn't appear to be anyone home."

"Let's find the telephone," Lamb said impatiently, and stepped through into the room to the left. Inside was a dining room table. A single setting of dirty dishes was present. The partially eaten remains of a chicken breast was affixed to the plate. A ceramic mug stood nearby. The doctor sniffed the contents and grimaced. "Stale beer," he said to Anna, who had followed him.

Passing through to the kitchen, they were greeted by O'Malley, who had gone through the room to the right of the door and entered an oddly neat kitchen from Lamb and Anna's right. Canisters stood on a countertop along the far wall on either side of a sink beneath a grimy window. Between the two doors stood an icebox. Immediately to the left of the dining room doorway was another counter, whose top was a dirty, wooden cutting board. A cleaver lay near a pan containing the carcass of a chicken.

Anna carefully put a finger to the pan. It was room temperature. Lamb examined the icebox. The ice inside was partially melted, but there was still a sizable block inside, such that it must have been replaced in the last few days.

"No sign of a telephone," the doctor said. "Did you see one in the other room?"

"No," O'Malley replied, "There are a pair of doorways down here." He indicated the short hallway he had come through.

One door contained a stairway down into the basement. Inside the other door was a small chamber with a chair and a table upon which rested a pad, pen, and a telephone. The priest put the receiver to his ear, tapped the arm on the base a few times, and frowned.

"The telephone isn't working," he told the others, returning it to the table. Lamb slapped himself on the forehead with his palm.

"If we couldn't call to here," he said in disgust, "why did we think we could call out?"

"Nevertheless," Anna said, "perhaps we can find tools that we can use to return Shane's car to the -" She stopped suddenly at a quiet thump from the basement. "Did you hear that?" she whispered. Lamb and O'Malley both nodded. The doctor drew his revolver from beneath his jacket, and Anna pulled hers from her waistband. Seeing the others armed, O'Malley opened his valise and drew the automatic. Lamb glanced to the others. Anna and O'Malley nodded, and the doctor led the way down the steps.

Chapter 4

July 16, 1929

Lamb descended the dark stairwell. The steps were steep, and creaked despite his slow, deliberate steps. Given all the noise that they had made upstairs, the doctor was sure that whoever, or whatever, was down there knew they were coming, but he proceeded with care out of habit. O'Malley had produced a flashlight from his valise, but its narrow beam did little to pierce the darkness while it advertised their location.

A few steps short of the bottom, right before the stairwell cleared the bottom of the ground floor, Lamb raised his hand and stopped. O'Malley walked absently into him, and the doctor sprawled on the floor at the base of the steps with a crash. The priest descended quickly to his side, shining the light on his colleague, when something struck his hand. The flashlight fell to the ground and disappeared out of sight.

Suddenly, Anna saw a blur as a hunched figure hit what she believed to be O'Malley on the back of the head. The priest fell on top of Lamb. Anna fired in the direction the blur had moved in. She heard the sound of a ricochet, and then there was silence.

"Who's there?" Anna heard a muffled voice say from farther into the darkness.

A moment later, a beam of light darted in all directions. Lamb had recovered the flashlight and was seeking out their assailant. Not finding anyone, he directed the beam onto O'Malley, who was sprawled face down. Anna descended quickly to his side, and saw a bloody gash in the back of head. Lamb knelt beside her and gave Anna the flashlight. Then he examined the priest's head, wiping the wound clean with his handkerchief. He pointed at Anna's necktie. She set her pistol and the flashlight down on the step with the beam pointing toward O'Malley and started to remove the tie with her free hand.

No sooner had she released hold of the gun than a disheveled, hunched man in a pair of stained overalls appeared with a fire poker in his hand intent on striking Lamb. Before Anna could alert him, she was deafened by the report of O'Malley's automatic. The assailant screeched, dropped his weapon, and fell to the ground clutching his shattered knee. Lamb turned to the man and punched him several times in the face until he stopped moving.

Lamb wiped his bloody fist on the man's shirt before returning to O'Malley and placing a hand gently on his back to keep him from moving. Then he accepted Anna's necktie and tied the wadded handkerchief into place over the priest's wound.

"Hello, out there," the voice said. "There's no need for stealth. We are quite alone here now. That miscreant is the only soul for miles. If you've vanquished that fiend, you've earned yourself a respite."

In the center of the room was a low stone table. On the far side of the chamber was a covered well. Along one wall were racks of stout shelves containing dozens of what looked like smooth, metallic, gallon-sized paint cans bearing strange symbols. Each one had numerous sockets of different shapes along the surface. On the wall to the side of the entrance was a table, upon which sat two of the can-like devices. Several oddly-shaped attachments were plugged into the sockets of each.

As she stared at the devices, she was startled as a segmented, antenna-like appliance on one of the kegs bent in her direction, revealing mechanical lenses that focused on her. Another convex attachment bore numerous, small convex protrusions that blinked sporadically in various colors. A third resembled four long, rectangular trumpets, arranged in two pairs side-by-side, also attached to the base by a segmented, antenna-like appliance.

"**Good day, miss,**" came a staccato monotone from the trumpet-like devices of the canister that was "looking" at her as lights blinked in unison from the convex attachment.

◆

"Hello?" Anna said tentatively to the device.

"**Hello,**" it replied in the same staccato monotone with corresponding lights. The harsh quality of the sound caused her neck to tense and an uncomfortable sensation to form behind her eyes. "**Have you dispatched Billy?**"

"If you mean the man who attacked us," Anna replied guardedly, "I do not believe that he is dead." She shone the flashlight about the room.

"**There is a light switch to your right,**" the voice said.

Anna flipped the switch, and the chamber was revealed. She could see now that the table was stained with blood. There was a trail of red leading to and over the lip of the well. The "paint cans" on the shelf appeared identical except for one, which had a different arrangement of sockets.

The device that was "speaking" to her sat on its table next to another one, but the latter had only the convex attachment plugged in, and no lights flashed. On the other side of the communicative container was a chessboard where a game had been in progress. The black player, whose pieces were nearest the device, was winning. There was a chair on the other side of the board, possibly where their attacker, Billy, had been the white player.

"I'm afraid you'll have to be my opponent now," the voice said. "If you would reset the board, we can begin anew." At that moment, Lamb entered the chamber, followed by O'Malley.

"By all that's holy," the priest said, covering his mouth and nose as he looked over the bloody table. Anna had not noticed the smell of the place, but seeing the father's reaction brought it to her attention and she withdrew a handkerchief from her purse.

"That smells like embalming fluid," Lamb said. "But whoever was doing the work must have botched it." Then he noticed the well. "I bet he dropped his failures in there."

"Actually," the staccato voice said, "the Junazhi are most adroit in the surgical arts." Lamb jumped, and O'Malley backed into and fell over the chair at the sound of the voice. "But you are correct. They dissected their subjects expertly, and discarded those deemed inadequate to their interests in the well." It paused. "I imagine that I should be grateful to the Junazhi for not providing me with olfactory facilities."

"You," Anna said with a pause, "are human?"

"Of course," the voice said. Then it added, "Please forgive my lack of manners. You have no idea who I am. My name is Ambrose Gwinnett Bierce, and I'm a writer for William Randolph Hearst's newspapers."

"Ambrose Bierce?" Lamb said with disbelief. "He was killed in Mexico fifteen years ago! Murdered by Pancho Villa!"

"Poppycock," Bierce said flatly. "The Junazhi caught me and brought me here just yesterday."

"Bierce's body was never found," O'Malley said.

"And it still hasn't been," Lamb replied. He started looking around for wires leading out of the room. "The walls are too thick, and we're underground here, so it can't be a wireless signal. Where are you transmitting from?"

"You confound me," Bierce said. "I am present here on the table next to Kovacs."

"Meyer Kovacs?" Anna said with suspicion.

"Why yes," the voice said. "Are you acquainted?"

"I am renting his house," Anna replied. "He also disappeared. In 1916."

"So where, and when, do we find ourselves now?"

"Today is Tuesday, July 16, 1929," O'Malley said, and reached into his pocket for the stub of his train ticket. Anna guided his hand over so the paper was in front of the lens attachment. "You are outside of Chatham, New York on the estate of a Dr. Martin Langford.

"Some kind of barbaric surgery was done here," Lamb said, examining the table. "There's no way anyone could have survived. Unless this blood came from several people."

"While the Junazhi do appear to be barbaric in their methods," Bierce said, "their subjects do not suffer. I have witnessed many such procedures. And if what you say is true, and I have been in this state for fifteen years, our minds have been sustained within these devices without any kind of maintenance for quite some time."

◆

"What do you mean *'our minds'?!*" Lamb asked with surprise.

"Almost all of these devices contain extracted brains," Bierce replied in his staccato monotone.

"And they're human?" O'Malley said.

"Most of them," Bierce said. "The one on the lower shelf with the additional sockets is something else."

"And they are all 'alive'?" Anna asked.

"Yes, though Kovacs here has been inert since the procedure, and Teplow has been unresponsive."

"Brian Teplow," Anna asked.

"Yes, I believe that is how he was introduced."

"Where is he?" Lamb demanded.

"He is in the device on the right side on the middle shelf." O'Malley picked up the chair he had fallen over and slumped into it aghast.

Lamb glanced to the rack and noted three of the canisters on the middle shelf. The one on the left was the one with the extra sockets. The one in the middle and the one to the right were identical except for some kind of hieroglyphics etched into the surface. There were three canisters on the lower shelf, as well, and Lamb noted that one was coated in a slimy residue. The other two, which bore no hieroglyphics, were open at the top, and empty.

When Lamb reached forward to swipe a sample of the leaking fluid with his finger, the voice said, "Don't touch that. It is most unpleasant, if Billy's reaction was representative."

Lamb withdrew his hand. "What happened?" he asked.

"There was a flash, and it appeared to burn his skin," was the response.

"Some kind of electric shock, then," Lamb conjectured. "And that is what is inside the container?"

"So it would seem," Anna said.

"You said that Brian Teplow has been unresponsive since," O'Malley said, then paused to shudder before continuing. "his brain was deposited in that container?"

"That is correct."

"And when was that?" O'Malley asked.

"It is impossible to measure time accurately in here, but the Junazhi have returned three times since then."

"The things that did this have come back?" O'Malley said with alarm.

"Of course," Bierce said. "This is their covert. They gallivant for some time and return. Billy was installed to maintain their privacy in their absence. Sometimes they return with a new subject."

"And how long have they been gone?" Anna asked.

"We have played approximately fifty-three games of chess, which is fewer than we usually complete between their visits," Bierce mused, "but Billy's skill has improved over time. I expect that they should return soon."

Lamb returned the canister to the shelf and tentatively lifted the one identified as Brian Teplow. It was noticeably heavier than the other. The container was sealed with no evidence that the top had ever been missing. There were no seams and the entire surface, save for the sockets and the hieroglyphics engraved on the side, was smooth.

"How do we know that Brian is in here," Lamb said with frustration, "and still alive?"

"You could connect the receptors and try to communicate with him," Bierce replied, "I'm sure Kovacs won't mind. But as I said, Teplow has not been responsive since the procedure."

Lamb placed the canister on the chess board, knocking the pieces aside.

"That was not necessary," Bierce said.

Lamb examined the attachments on Kovacs' canister. "Do I simply unplug them and insert them in the corresponding socket?" he asked. "Or is there a switch or something to enable the transfer."

"Simply remove them from Kovacs and insert them in the appropriate receptacle."

"Which is the auditory device?" Lamb asked. Bierce guided the doctor in removing the devices from Kovacs and inserting it into Brian's container. As soon as he connected the first attachment, the convex device, the tension and discomfort that the newcomers had experienced returned, increased significantly. Anna swooned, but caught herself, descended gracefully, and sat on the concrete floor. O'Malley grasped his head in his hands and leaned forward in anguish. Lamb persevered, and when the final convex attachment was connected, the sensations dropped to a tolerable level. One of the lights blinked intermittently.

"What does that light mean?" Lamb asked.

"I believe it means that young Brian's mind is active," Bierce replied, "but not conscious. Perhaps he is dreaming."

"Do we risk waking him up?" Anna asked as she slowly rose to her feet and leaned on the table. "It is said that waking people while dreaming is extremely traumatic."

"And we have no idea what condition he might be in, in this state," Lamb agreed.

"So there are six of these containers," O'Malley said with renewed vigor. "And this-thing, who claims to be famed journalist, Ambrose Bierce-"

"You flatter me, sir," Bierce said with the same emotionless monotone.

"This thing," O'Malley continued, "claims that three of them contain preserved and functional human brains, while the other has some kind of unknown being in it?!" He shook his head. "By all that is righteous and just, if these wild assertions are true, we should release these poor souls from immortal torment!"

"**That is preposterous,**" the staccato monotone and Lamb said in unison.

"If these people-" Lamb started.

"If they can still be considered people," O'Malley interrupted.

"If these people are truly alive," Lamb continued, "in some form, then we must study them and learn how this was done!" O'Malley shook his head vigorously. "Think of the medical advancements that could be derived from this research! Millions of lives could be saved with this technology."

"And what sort of life is it?" O'Malley retorted. "A mind with no physical form? Does that even count as human?" He paused for breath. "And what of that other thing," he said pointing at the unusually configured canister on the shelf. "With their physical form, humanity and whatever that is are indistinguishable."

"**Would that not be beneficial to human, and interspecies relations?**" Bierce asked. "**Does is not say in** *Romans* '**live in harmony with one another. Repay no one evil for evil'?**"

"At the very least," Lamb said, "we need to first determine if there are human minds encased in these cans, and if so, what mental state that they are in."

"**I assure you,**" Bierce said, "**that there is no sensation of pain. And after the initial adjustment, no feelings of loss or misfortune.**"

"Do you still feel your body?" Lamb asked. "It's called Phantom Limb Syndrome. It was quite common among amputees during the Great War."

"There will be time for these philosophical discussions later," Anna interjected. "But right now, we need to determine what to do with Brian Teplow. We clearly can't take him to his moth-"

"Did you hear that?" O'Malley said after shushing the others.

"I did not hear anything," Anna replied.

"I heard howling," O'Malley said, "but it stopped."

"The Junazhi have returned."

Chapter 5

July 16, 1929

A palpable feeling of confined dread filled the basement chamber as three semi-transparent beings passed incorporeally through the wall nearest the well before solidifying. They were human-sized, but had long, gnarled, bulbous bodies crowned by a spherical head bearing innumerable stalks that glowed intermittently. They had five pairs of segmented, insect-like legs that ended in dexterous claws with three fingers that extended radially from each leg.

O'Malley recognized them as the things painted on the reliquary box that he had been given in Rome.

The front right leg of one of the things held a metallic wand. The other two beings carried Shane and Cletus, who appeared to be frozen.

At the sight of Anna's group, the stalks of each of the three new arrivals started to blink in rapid, sporadic, chaotic patterns. To Anna's surprise, the convex appliance attached to Bierce's container flashed in a similar manner. They were communicating. Anna, Lamb, and O'Malley stood motionless, mesmerized by the display.

"**These are the Junazhi,**" Bierce said. "**They captured these spies nearby.**" The bulbous entities stalks continued to flash as he spoke.

"That man and his dog brought us here," Lamb said. "What's happened to them?"

"**They have been frozen,**" Bierce replied. "**Fear not. The Junazhi would not dispatch them outright. They require live brains for the extraction process.**"

"You mean that they intend to take their brains and put them in those containers?" O'Malley said.

"**That is their quandary,**" Bierce said. "**They had intended to harvest the minds of these spies, but they find yours' far more interesting.**"

"Our brains, and theirs for that matter," indicating Shane and Cletus, "are not for them to take. We mean the Junazhi no harm. We just came to bring Brian Teplow home." At the mention of the name, the Junazhi turned toward Anna. Their stalks flickered more quickly, causing a blinding, almost strobe-like effect.

Suddenly, Lamb opened fire with his pistol at the nearest one. The bullets seemed to pass right through and struck the wall behind it. The lead Junazhi pointed the device at Lamb, and a colorless, but visible cloud was projected from the tip. Lamb froze in place the instant the cloud struck him.

A moment later, O'Malley aimed the relic, which he had retrieved from his valise, and willed a beam at the alien shooter. It came out brilliant orange, and the Junazhi disintegrated. The father pointed his device in the direction of the other two.

"Tell them to release their prisoners and move away," O'Malley said, keeping his focus, and aim, squarely on the bulbous beings. Bierce's device flashed a rapid-fire pattern. The beings dropped Shane and Cletus, who fell to the ground and shattered like fine crystal. The dog's head wobbled across the floor and stopped at Anna's feet.

◆

The lights of Bierce's attachment and the stalks flashed rapidly, with most of the flashes coming from Bierce.

Anna was dumbstruck at the sight of the dog's face at her feet. The large brown eyes were frozen in place and pointed toward her. She stifled a gasp and forced herself to maintain her neutral expression. These Junazhi clearly only understood literal communication with them.

O'Malley was horrified as he glanced at the shards that were clearly pieces of Shane scattered across the concrete floor, and also at the effect the relic had had on the alien. He had willed the beam, but what would happen had been unknown.

"They can be restored," Bierce's staccato monotone eventually said. "I have tried to explain to the Junazhi, as I have several times in the past, that human communication is always to be taken literally, but it is a concept that alludes them."

"Nevertheless, they are skilled surgeons that function in dimensions beyond human understanding, and they assure me that the subjects can be restored to their original state, though their value as experimental subjects has been eliminated."

"Then tell them to 'reassemble' our friends," O'Malley said, thrusting the relic in the direction of the aliens menacingly. "At once!"

Bierce's lights flashed and then the stalks of the aliens joined the light show.

◆

Anna jumped with a start. She and Lamb were seated in the chairs. Cletus sat on the floor between them, licking the doctor's hand. O'Malley stood on Anna's other side now, pointing the metal device that encased his left hand at the aliens. Several Junazhi faded in and out before them and around the table, but they all appeared identical, so it was unclear to Anna whether they were the same individuals or not.

She had been disarmed, and everything except her clothing had been taken, including her shoes. She was not restrained and did not seem to be injured in any way. She glanced at O'Malley and saw him suddenly animate, looking about as perplexed as she was. He and Lamb had also been relieved of their possessions, except for the device that the father held.

Billy, the man who had attacked them at the bottom of the stairs, stood next to the nearest shelves bearing the canisters. The knee that the priest had shot showed no signs of injury. Anna recognized her handbag, O'Malley's valise, and their shoes laying on the top shelf. Billy was admiring the father's automatic. Anna's revolver and Lamb's pistol were tucked into the man's waistband.

One of the aliens solidified before them. Cletus growled and took up a defensive posture between the seated people and the Junazhi. It seemed to ignore the dog. Its head stalks flashed rapidly. The Bierce container was on the table behind Anna and O'Malley, but Anna could feel pulses as its attachment flashed in response.

"What just happened?" Anna asked, still unsure of her condition.

"What do you mean?" O'Malley asked. "I didn't see anything."

"Then how did I end up in this chair," Anna replied, "with that once shattered creature sitting at my feet?"

"I don't understand the science," the monotone staccato said too loudly, "but the Junazhi perceive past, present, and future concurrently. To your eyes, they seem to appear and disappear. That is simply your mind trying to make sense of achronological travel."

"You mean that they travel across all moments," Anna said, pausing to make sense of her thought. "At the same time?"

"That is correct, and they brought you, Dr. Rykov, with them between the jumps that you perceive."

"I didn't notice anything," O'Malley said, still perplexed.

"That device on your hand is from their dimension. Somehow, you did not perceive the transit. You must be connected to their plane of existence through it."

"That must be why it affected the one I hit," O'Malley said, "when Harry's bullets could not."

"And also why Billy could relieve you of it. It has the Junazhi quite concerned."

"What about Harry?" Anna asked with concern. The doctor's ashen complexion made him appear like stone, though his skin was warm and normal when Anna touched his cheek.

"The Junazhi have trapped him between dimensions. To him, time is standing still."

"Are they helping Shane?" Anna asked.

"As you can see," Bierce continued, "the Junazhi were able to reassemble the dog. They are prepared to do the same for the other spy if you will perform an errand for them."

"Why us?" O'Malley asked.

"Not all of you. Just Dr. Rykov."

"Then why me?" Anna asked.

"You have a connection to Meyer Kovacs. It transcends existences, and you would be able to contact him."

"I thought you said that Kovacs was dead," O'Malley said accusingly.

"I said that Kovacs' mind was inert. There has been no activity from his brain. His mind fled when he was harvested. The Junazhi know where he is, but are unable to interact with him there."

"What do you mean *'his mind fled'*," O'Malley asked.

"Through some means that I do not understand, Kovacs was able to escape to another existence, where he was able to establish a permanent presence."

"And what of Brian Teplow?" Anna asked.

"Kovacs somehow took Teplow's mind with him, but it is still linked to the young man's brain."

"What do they want me to do?"

"The Junazhi want you to travel to the plane where Kovacs now resides and destroy his presence there. When that occurs, they believe that his mind will be restored to his brain."

"Where he would be trapped in one of those canisters as you are," O'Malley said in disgust.

"Why would I want to facilitate Kovacs' imprisonment by the Junazhi?" Anna asked

"Allow me to assure you that my existence is not unpleasant. In fact, there is no emotion, no discomfort, and no idleness or boredom. Freed of my physical confines, and with the technologies that the Junazhi have provided me, my mind has been able to expand beyond the confines of human understanding."

"What Kovacs has done, as I understand it, is to weaken the barriers between the innumerable planes of existence. Not just one, mind you, but just as the Junazhi exist simultaneously essentially everywhere, all the planes are inexorably linked to each other. He may not even be aware of the peril that he has put all of existence in."

"And what of Brian Teplow?" Anna asked.

"If you go to the realm that Kovacs created, you should be able to make contact with him."

"What will happen to Brian if Kovacs is killed in that other realm?" Anna asked. There was a pause as Bierce and various Junazhi communicated.

"The Junazhi believe that his mind will also return to his brain."

"So Brian would also be trapped in one of those cans," O'Malley said.

"That is correct."

"And what will happen to Anna?" O'Malley asked.

"Her body is still intact. Her mind would be restored to it."

"What do you mean *'her mind would be restored to her body'*?" O'Malley said, pointing the gauntlet toward the Junazhi.

"To facilitate the transport, it would be most efficient to transplant Dr. Rykov's brain into one of the cylinders-"

"That's not going to happen!" O'Malley interrupted.

"You said that that was the most efficient means," Anna interjected. "Is there another way?"

Bierce relayed the question and received a response. "The Junazhi say that the transport could be accomplished chemically, but that method is not as reliable." He received more flashes from the aliens. "It is possible that your mind could become detached in the other realm and not find its way back to your current existence."

"And you say that, if I make this journey, I might be able to speak with Brian?"

"That is correct."

"How does that help us?" O'Malley asked Anna incredulously.

"We could learn what he told Longborough," she replied.

"What does that even matter now?" the priest said. "We've crossed paths with demons, gods, and aliens. What difference will knowing what Brian told Longborough make now? It was probably about all of this, and Brian went with Kovacs to escape."

"There is only one way to find out," Anna said with finality. "I will go."

Chapter 6

July 16, 1929

As soon as Anna spoke the words, O'Malley saw a Junazhi materialize behind her and poke a finger from its front claws into each of her ears. Anna's body stiffened, and she sat up straight. There was an audible snap, and her body went slack An instant later, the being appeared behind Lamb and performed the same procedure. Immediately after the snap, the doctor's ashen complexion returned to something resembling normal, and he slumped into his chair.

O'Malley was tempted to fire upon the thing, but hesitated for fear of hitting Anna or Lamb, and then the alien faded away again. Before their assailant had completely disappeared, Anna started convulsing, the veins in her head visibly throbbing, and she slipped off the chair to the floor.

"What's happening?" O'Malley cried, sliding to his knees at her side. Bierce's lights flashed, though the priest did not see the Junazhi he communicated with.

"She is reacting to the Junazhi serum. They say that her chemistry has been previously altered by a similar compound."

"What does that mean?!"

"The outcome is uncertain."

O'Malley scowled, removed his cassock, and folded it into a ball under her head. The relic had obligingly shrunk to pass through the sleeve, but was still affixed to his left hand. He glanced to Lamb. The doctor remained motionless in his chair.

"Why did they inject the doctor?" O'Malley asked accusingly. "That was not part of the arrangement."

"He has been modified so that the Junazhi can monitor Dr. Rykov's progress. His reaction to the procedure is the expected outcome."

As they spoke, Anna's spasms subsided, and her expression calmed. O'Malley thought he noticed goosebumps on her arms for a brief moment.

"How can they keep track of Anna?"

"It is difficult to explain, but suffice it to say that they can perceive through his sensory organs."

"So they can see what Lamb sees, hear what he hears, smell what he smells, and so on?"

"Not exactly. The Junazhi perceive differently from humans. But they will be able to experience what he does."

"Can they arrange for me to see as well?" Bierce's lights flashed again. This time O'Malley stayed alert with the relic ready, but no assailant appeared.

"You can be implanted with sensory augmentation to enable visual reception." O'Malley tensed.

"Is there an external means to this end?" After another illuminated dialog, Billy stepped out of the chamber, still carrying their guns. The man had been so silent and still that the priest had forgotten he was there.

◆

Harry Lamb reclined comfortably on the settee of the bedchamber Queen Sif had allocated to him. He wore a long kilt, a thin linen shirt, and simple sandals. He had nodded off, probably on account of the excellent wine his assigned servant, Shemei, had piled him with.

Lamb was not sure how he had gotten to the palace. He had no memory of anything since he, Father O'Malley, and Anna Rykov had left the Oak Valley Sanitarium. The first thing he remembered was being escorted into a throne room that reminded him of the palace at Versailles. He had visited it with Annette while on leave during the Great War. The memory brought a smile to his face.

The guards uncrossed their pole weapons to allow the footman to open the door. The sight of Liv Lee, the same sexy actress he had met in New York only a few weeks ago, made his heart jump. She sat upon a red, velvet throne atop a three-stepped dais in a tight, golden dress, studded with pearls and gems, and an Egyptian-style crown. From behind her, children with shiny skin toddled into view before being herded into an antechamber behind the throne by waiting maidens.

She was now Queen Sif of Brynner, ruler of the Isle of Brynn. Lamb thought he had lost her when the gigantic avatar of Utgarda had grasped her in its giant red trunk and threw her off into an extra-dimensional landscape that had subsequently disappeared.

The queen had acknowledged his entry into the room with a cursory nod, but then looked again with a glint of recognition in her eyes. The footman approached a courtier holding a long, gold-inlaid staff of dark wood and whispered something to him.

"My Queen," the courtier shouted, "a vagrant collected in the marketplace claims that you and he are acquainted. Per your instructions, he had been brought to your royal presence for an interview. He calls himself Harry Lamb."

"Has he been mistreated in any way?" the queen asked.

"No, my Queen," the footman said after a bow. "After he announced your acquaintance, and the guards mentioned your name, the subject came voluntarily."

"And what is he wearing?" the queen said scornfully. Lamb noted that he was dressed in a worn leather shirt and trousers, his feet were bare, and he looked as if he had been living in a pig sty.

"Harry Lamb was brought directly to you," the footman said, "per your orders. Your instructions did not state the nature of your interest-"

"He could have been cleaned up first," the queen interrupted. She scanned the room. "You," the queen shouted, pointing to a pretty blond girl dressed in a see-through dress that wrapped tightly around her body.

"Shemei, my queen," the servant said with a curtsy.

"Get him cleaned up, into some proper clothes, and fed. I will interview him later." Then she snapped her fingers, and Lamb, the servant, and the two guards followed the footman out another door. The short hallway ended in another door. The footman lingered for a moment before it, and then pulled it open with a flourish.

The footman and the servant followed Lamb into the room. Lamb spun around admiring the large bed, wardrobes, and the writing desk and chairs. There were several full-size portraits of the queen. As he admired them, for a brief moment the elegant gowns and uniforms became skimpy and suggestive and the elegant, stately woman's torso appeared as part of the enormous body of some kind of insect. But when he blinked his eyes the portraits returned to normal. Feeling dizzy, he collapsed onto the bed.

"This will be your quarters until the queen calls for you," the footman said with authority. Then he turned, without a word, gave a firm gaze at the servant, who curtsied, and left the room. The door closed behind him.

The servant started to undress Lamb. He stopped her reflexively. The woman shrugged and pointed to a small pool that Lamb had not noticed in a far corner. She then stepped toward the pool herself, seductively removing her own clothing step by step. She stopped at the edge of the water, and turned to him, completely naked, with her hands on her hips.

"You must be presentable when the queen calls for you," the servant said. "You do not want to make her angry." Lamb hesitated. "If she is displeased with you," the woman said, "she will sate her anger on me." She appeared to say more, but Lamb could not understand the words.

◆

Anna found herself in the dark. She was cold. She pulled her knees to her chest and wrapped her arms around them only to discover that she was naked, and that her wrists were bound together in irons linked by a foot or so of thick chain and connected to similar shackles around her ankles, as well as to a ring in the floor.

A moment of panic flooded through her as she took in the situation. She was sitting atop a small pile of limp straw over the hard stone floor. In the distance she could hear the quiet sobbing of men and women. The smells of sweat, fear, and human waste permeated her surroundings. A hint of light came from a thin slit at the bottom of what she thought was a door.

Anna tried to stand, but collapsed as a throbbing in the center of her head overcame her, and she settled back onto the straw. Then she heard movement nearby. The clinking of her chains had alerted another occupant of the cell who had previously been silent.

"Hello?" Anna said tentatively. "Is someone there?" The movement stopped, but Anna detected the sound of metal scraping slowly on stone a few feet to her right. She turned toward the sound and squinted as her eyes adjusted to the dim light.

The other being seemed to be accustomed to the conditions already. It waited until Anna's eyes made out its shape, and then lunged toward her. Anna screamed, but the prisoner fell forward as its shackled leg went taut against the ring set into the floor. Still it clawed at Anna, trying to loop the chain between its wrists around Anna's foot. But the chain attached to the manacles had been precisely measured so that she was mere inches out of reach.

As her vision focused, Anna could discern that the other prisoner was a large but emaciated man. He was shackled against the opposite wall of the cell, where the chain of his leg irons passed through the heavy ring in the floor. He had a mop of stringy hair, and his fingers ended with long, gnarled nails that were cracked and jagged. The man growled, but made no comprehensible sounds.

The sound of slow, deliberate footsteps approached the door. There was a rumble of keys, and the cell was flooded with the light of a single torch. Two muscular, humanoid creatures entered the cell. One held the torch. The other carried a long staff with a claw-like device at one end and a spearhead on the other. Both wore Roman-style armor, complete with arm and leg guards. But their heads were those of insects. They had large, bulbous, compound eyes and wide, curved mandibles jutting out of their cheeks to meet in front of narrow pointed beaks. Nevertheless, something about the two looked familiar.

It was clear that the torch was for the benefit of the prisoners. The guards looked about, regardless of where the light shined. The one with the staff twisted the handle, the device opened, and he grabbed the man around the neck. The man screamed as the claw snapped shut. The guard threw the man against the wall, expertly releasing the claw so the prisoner flew into the wall and landed face down against it.

The other guard set the torch down on the floor in a specific spot so that the entirely of the chamber was exposed. The cell was maybe ten feet square, composed of stone slabs. There were no windows or openings of any kind except the door. Six rings were set in the floor; two on each of the walla facing the door. Anna and the man were set diagonally across from each other, with him closer to the door. The man was also naked, and his body was covered in all manner of scars. His prominent ribs indicated that he had not eaten properly in a very long time. Noting the lack of straw, Anna conjectured that he may have eaten it.

The guard pulled Anna to her feet and waited for her to take stock of her situation. When she turned toward him, he grasped her chin with a human hand and pulled her close enough to gently hold her face down with the pointed tips of his mandibles. She then watched as he pawed all over her body, stopping in strategic places that he knew made Anna uncomfortable, the torchlight ensuring that she could see what he was doing. He was asserting his total power over her. Eventually, he released Anna's head and pushed her backward onto the straw.

"Tell the queen she is awake," the guard said as he picked up the torch. Then the two stepped out, the door closed, and a key jostled in the lock too many times before the footsteps faded away slowly and deliberately.

◆

Lamb was just about to nod off again when the door to the chamber opened and the footman entered.

"The Queen will see you now," he snapped as if to a subordinate.

Lamb stood casually and started to straighten his clothes, but Shemei slapped away his hands, knelt in front of him, and arranged his wardrobe herself.

"Must make a good impression," she said in a chirpy tone with a note of nervousness.

"I'm sure everything will be fine," Lamb said with a reassuring smile. Shemei blushed and turned away. When she rose, the footman grasped the doctor's arm and ushered him quickly out the door, where the two guards with the halberds that had escorted him to the room were waiting. They followed as the footman led Lamb down the short hallway and into the throne room.

Chapter 7

Dhath Gl'clot 11

He was brought to the end of a long red carpet that led up the dais and under the throne.

"That is much better." Queen Sif smiled as he bowed. "I would know the reason for your presence in Brynner, Harry Lamb."

"Your Majesty," Lamb said with a knowing grin, "I don't know how I got here, or why, but my colleague and I were searching for a mystic named Brian Teplow." The queen scowled.

"Deb-Roh!" she shouted. "You seek Deb-Roh?!"

"Yes, your Majesty," Lamb replied. "He may be known by that name here."

"Deb-Roh is a sorcerer and a scoundrel. Why do you wish to find him?"

"My colleague is the one who seeks information from him?"

"And who is this colleague?"

"Dr. Anna Rykov. But I do not know if she is here. As I said, I don't know how I got here myself."

Harry glanced from side to side nervously. Perhaps he was mistaken. The queen looked exactly like Liv Lee, and she seemed to know him, at least on some level, but clearly she did not remember their prior relationship.

The queen gazed at Lamb for a long moment. Everyone in the throne room was silent and motionless. Finally she smiled and motioned toward a settee to the right of the dais.

"Recline and restore yourself," she said in a tone Lamb could not decide was sensual or predatory. "We will consider your quest in due time." She clapped her hands and Shemei appeared quickly from the shadows. "Attend to him."

The servant curtsied, and the queen watched her ominously as she stepped around the throne and knelt at Lamb's side. When Shemei had settled, the queen nodded at the courtier with the staff.

◆

Anna's eyes had adjusted to the dimness of the cell. The man imprisoned with her had continued growling at her, and had tried again a few times to reach her, but the measurements of their bonds had been precise. The guards had not returned, in spite of the noise, for several hours. But similar noises were coming from beyond the door.

She had fallen asleep at some point, because she was rudely awakened by a pressure around her neck. She opened her eyes to see one of the insect-men holding the pole device. The other unlocked the ring in the floor to release her leg irons. She was pulled to her feet by the device while the other prisoner leered and made rude noises. When standing, the shackles prevented Anna from raising her hands above her waist.

The other guard picked up a similar device, which he had leaned against the wall, and grasped the man's neck in his claw. The man instantly froze and went silent, his eyes wide before the guard twisted the staff and the claw snapped. The man's head was cut clean off and rolled across the floor before the body fell forward.

"You are being taken before the queen," the guard said. "Behave yourself, or you will suffer the same fate." He did not wait for a reply before he walked out of the cell. Anna was pushed through the door by the guard holding the pole behind her. Her leg shackles echoed as they led her along a winding, circular corridor that sloped upward. Windowless doors lined both sides.

Anna had grown accustomed to the cold, but the wetness made her bare feet numb. She avoided the lewd gazes of the insect-man guards that were posted along the corridor and plodded on. The stone steps had been worn practically into a ramp, and the damp surroundings made them slippery. Twice she slipped and nearly choked as the guard with the claw pulled her to her feet.

Eventually they reached the end of the corridor. The lead guard tapped on the heavy wooden door with his staff, and it opened from the other side. A wave of warm air swept over Anna's naked body as she was prodded out of the dungeon and across a stone-flagged courtyard. The tiles were hot and her feet burned with each step.

There were several humans wearing Egyptian-style clothing there. They were bare-chested with long skirts, and wore beaded collars that draped over their shoulders and chests. They had been in the midst of an animated conversation, but when Anna was brought by, they stopped the procession. The guard behind her used the claw to hold her still and pulled her up onto her toes. The assembly then examined her appraisingly, especially her eyes, ears, and teeth. Anna could not resist, and the guards did not interfere.

When they had finished their inspection, which appeared to have been disappointing, the men stepped away and resumed their conversation. Anna was returned to her feet and pushed forward again.

At the far end of the courtyard two insect-man guards with the clawed pole weapons stood in front of a pair of huge doors that each bore a bas relief of Liv Lee dressed as Cleopatra.

◆

Anna and Lamb had been unresponsive for over an hour. O'Malley watched over the two in case the aliens decided to try and remove their brains after all.

"Why haven't they attacked me?" O'Malley asked, standing vigil over the slumped bodies of his friends. "I vaporized one of them, and they have ignored me ever since."

"The Junazhi are timeless," Bierce replied. **"From your perspective, they can wait you out."**

"So they already know the outcome of this adventure?"

"While I can communicate with them, the Junazhi and I do not share thoughts. I don't know their motivations or intentions."

During this time, Billy went to the main room of the guest house basement and returned with odd, seemingly unrelated junk. He operated absently, as if externally controlled, which O'Malley imagined he was.

As he cobbled together the disparate parts, other devices phased into view on the table, and Billy integrated them into the contraption.

Finally, Billy sat on the table next to the device. He then plugged in a thick cable ending in a probe with a pair of bulbous tips, which he unceremoniously thrust up his nose. Billy's body stiffened, and a hazy image appeared on a pane of glass.

"That is Dr. Lamb's visual sensory input." They saw that Lamb was lying on a couch and was being hand fed by a woman who his attention was completely focused on. The woman wore a thin linen dress. Behind her was a large room with many humanoid shapes standing around. To O'Malley, a professor of Ancient History, the architecture appeared to be Ancient Egyptian, as was the woman's outfit.

Lamb's view followed the woman's gaze to a blurry female shape sitting on a throne.

"Why is that woman so indistinct?" Bierce's lights flashed.

"The Junazhi say that something is confusing Dr. Lamb's senses. The device cannot clearly distinguish the reality from the illusion."

Suddenly there was a commotion as a door at the far end of the chamber opened.

◆

Anna hobbled into an ornate chamber filled with people in Egyptian-style dress. The human men wore the long, white kilts, some with shirts underneath and others bare-chested. Most of the women, who were all human, wore poncho-like dresses of plain white. All wore colorful, beaded collars that draped over their shoulders and chests. Some of the human men and women, who were clearly slaves, wore simple, form-fitting, translucent costumes. Scattered around the perimeter of the room were insect-man guards dressed in scale armor vests, with arm and leg protectors. Each held the clawed pole weapon, though some also had oddly shaped swords.

The room was dark, illuminated only by strategically placed skylights that focused attention on an open space in the center of the room, and on a raised dais bearing a throne. And on that throne sat Liv Lee. She was dressed in a tight, ornately decorated, wrap-around dress that appeared to be woven of gold. On her head was a golden circlet studded with jewels, and in the front, over her forehead, was a representation of the tentacle-faced avatar of Utgarda.

Anna was prodded toward the illuminated space before the dais and made to kneel with her forehead touching the floor.

"My queen," an insect-man courtier shouted to the assembly after tapping the gilded staff of a seneschal on the tile floor three times, "the conspirator, Nygof, has been apprehended and is brought before you." Anna tried to look up, but the claw kept her head on the floor.

"So, Nygof," Liv said in a haughty and commanding voice, "I finally have you in chains. You will tell me of Deb-Roh's plot, the names of your co-conspirators, and how you managed to get into the palace." She sneered cruelly. "But first, let me get a good look at you,"

As the queen moved forward, Anna noticed that what had looked like the throne was actually the pattern on an enormous, slug-like body. The parody of Liv Lee bore the forward appearance of the actress, but as soon as she moved, Anna could see that the image was a pattern in her fleshy surface. In her wake, barely visible behind the enormous bulk, were pale, white larvae, glistening with slime, but having two arms and two legs.

Anna was about to react when the pressure around her neck increased slightly as a warning. As the queen stepped down from her throne, Anna suddenly noticed Lamb lying on a couch to the side of the throne. He was dressed in the same clothing as the other men, and a woman was sitting next to him feeding him, dressed in a translucent garment that covered her from neck to ankles. The doctor was fully fixated on her.

Anna′s gaze was abruptly turned by the queen′s hand on her chin so they were eye to eye. Liv′s face bore an expression of malice and disgust. She sneered as she lifted Anna by the chin to her feet and circled her to admire the naked body in chains.

"You have no disguise to conceal your true identity now, Nygof. And if you're still alive when I am finished with you, you won′t have to hide because no one will want to look upon you again!"

Chapter 8

July 16, 1929

O'Malley gasped as he saw Anna, naked and in chains, pushed into the chamber by a blurry humanoid holding her by the neck in a mancatcher.

"What the devil is going on here?" O'Malley shouted. "You sent them off together. Why have they been separated?" Bierce's lights flashed.

"The Junazhi hypothesize that the chemical interference from Dr. Rykov's prior contamination caused her to be rerouted to an unfavorable existence, while Dr. Lamb was deposited in a more fortunate circumstance."

"What do you mean 'an unfavorable existence' and 'a more fortunate circumstance'?"

"The existences that they are experiencing are in the mental realm of Brian Teplow. He created this existence, and Kovacs has commandeered it."

"How does that affect Anna and Harry's situations within it? Neither Brian nor Kovacs has ever met either of them." More flashes from Bierce.

"Their mental condition, as defined by their brain chemistry, significantly impacts how they will be represented. Dr. Lamb had a peaceful transition, while Dr. Rykov's reaction to the Junazhi injection was traumatic."

"And this is the result?" O'Malley asked. "We need to assist them somehow!"

"We are unable to interact with them," and as if reading O'Malley's thought, "and any interference with their bodies could cause serious mental and physical damage."

O'Malley was helpless to assist them. All he could do was watch events unfold. And unlike a silent movie, there were no narration cards to explain what was happening.

◆

Anna was reluctant to speak with the mancatcher holding her neck. The queen released her chin and turned to Lamb. "Harry Lamb! Attend me!"

Lamb gently pushed the servant aside, rose, and approached. Anna looked for some indication that he had a plan for getting out of this situation, but Lamb seemed surprised to see her and came to the queen's side.

"You, Nygof," Liv continued with scorn, "who would conspire with Deb-Roh and Gho-Bazh to depose me, see now how I possess all you owned." She embraced Lamb with tentacle-like arms and kissed him passionately on the lips while staring into her eyes. "And even your pitiful existence is mine to do with as I please." Lamb returned the embrace, his arm sinking into the gelatinous surface, but he did not appear to notice her monstrous form.

"Your Majesty," Lamb said when she released him, "this is my colleague, Dr. Anna Rykov. I think you have her confused with someone else."

"You are affiliated with Nygof?!" Liv cried, stepping away from the doctor. Two guards approached and pointed their mancatchers at him threateningly.

"No, your Majesty," Lamb said, holding his hands before him in a pacifying gesture. "Just as you confused me with this Nab person, you have imprisoned my associate by mistake. This is not Nygof. This is Anna Rykov." The queen looked skeptical.

"And what say you." When she noted that Anna was hesitant to speak, she gestured, and Anna was released from the mancatcher.

"It is as Dr. Lamb says," Anna said politely. "I am Dr. Anna Rykov. Dr. Lamb and I have been sent to dispatch Gho-Bazh and bring Deb-Roh home with us."

"It is not strange that you believe us to be others," Lamb said. "You, too, resemble someone we know from our home."

"My Queen. She was captured with the weapons and possessions said to be carried by Nygof," one of the guards said.

"I know who you are," the queen hissed so that only Anna could hear. "Anyone touched by Utgarda is irreversibly changed here. When I was thrown clear of the temple into the Endless Barrens of None, I became the parody you see before you. You are responsible for what has befallen me." She turned to the assembled courtiers and said, "Is there anything to suggest that she is who she claims to be?"

"No, my Queen," Govil replied immediately.

"You say you have been sent to kill Gho-Bazh," the queen said for all to hear. "You will perform this task. You will also bring Deb-Roh here to me, dead or alive." She looked to the guards who had brought Anna. "Guards!" They dropped to one knee and bowed their heads.

"Ganon," the one behind Anna said.

"Govil," the other replied.

"You will accompany Anna Rykov and see that she completes these tasks. If she should stray from my will, you will attend to her and then complete my instructions."

"Yes, my Queen," the guards replied in unison and stood.

"See that the expedition is properly equipped." She turned to the seneschal. "Draft an edict authorizing them to commandeer whatever they deem necessary to complete the assignment."

"Your Majesty," Lamb said as Liv climbed the steps to the top of the dais. "I will go with them to ensure that your instructions are carried out as you intend."

"Do not presume to command me, Harry Lamb," the Queen said, "but I will permit you to accompany them, chronicle their journey, and report back to me the details of this quest." She nodded to the seneschal, who tapped the floor with his staff.

"Your Maj-" Anna started to ask before the mancatcher was secured again around her neck and she was by prodded Ganon out of the throne room through a side door. Lamb was ushered back toward his room by Govil, with Shemei close behind as another matter was brought before the queen.

◆

"Release her at once," Lamb commanded after the door to his chamber closed. Govil scowled and pushed him onto the settee.

"First," the insect-man said evenly, "I don't answer to you. And second, she is still my prisoner. The Queen did not release her, so I may do as I please." At this, he stood behind

Anna and pressed his body against her back. Anna tried to squirm away, but was held her in place by the mancatcher.

"And you are here solely as an observer," Ganon added, "who doesn't need his liberty to perform his task."

"Well you can't expect me to complete the assignment naked and in chains," Anna said. "I will need all of my resources available to deal with things as they arise"

"I think all the resources you need are already available," Govil said, reaching around Anna to put his hand on her abdomen. Lamb moved to intervene, but stopped short as Ganon tightened the claw around her neck. "Let her go," Govil said. Ganon twisted the pole and the claw opened.

"Now, we need to get her some clothes-," Lamb said, but stopped short as Govil manhandled Anna face down onto the bed. Lamb shot up and punched the guard in the face before being struck in the back by Ganon. Govil was knocked aside into Shemei, and fell on top of her on the carpeted floor. He redirected his lust toward her, and she submitted to him as if accustomed to it.

Lamb doubled back at the impact and fell onto his back with the spear point of Ganon's mancatcher at his throat.

"As he said," the guard said, "you have no authority here. Even less than her. So mind your place." He lifted the spear and watched warily as Lamb rose to his knees and then to his feet.

In the meantime, Anna had rolled over and was sitting on the bed. She looked herself over in a full-sized mirror on a wall and noted that she appeared to be unharmed. She did not feel ill and, aside from Govil's predations, did not think she had been violated. However, she was quite dirty.

"I need to get cleaned up if I am to begin this journey," she said matter-of-factly. "I will stand out in a crowd like this."

Ganon eyed her up and down lasciviously, but then leaned his weapon against the wall and pressed a panel on his arm guard. Three very small keys emerged from slots in it. He drew each of them one at a time with his other hand and used all three to release the chains from Anna's cuffs.

"You can wash up over there," Lamb said loudly to be heard over the noise of Govil and Shemei. Anna glanced at the pool and followed his advice.

◆

"At least they are back together," O'Malley said. "Maybe they're getting directions to where Brian is."

"It would appear that they are making progress."

"It's still strange that some of the people are blurred for some reason, while others are not. What is so special about them?" Bierce's lights flashed.

"The Junazhi believe that those beings have been corrupted by Utgarda, and their true forms are incomprehensible to the human mind."

"But Harry doesn't seem to be repulsed."

"He can see the illusion that is being presented.

"The sooner this is done, the better."

◆

Some time later, Anna and Lamb were lying on the bed. Ganon and Govil watched them expressionlessly with their compound insect eyes. Anna had bathed, with the help of Shemei, who had joined her in the pool after her encounter with Govil. She showed Anna some lotions and cremes to cleanse herself with.

Anna now wore a rough vest and pants made of animal hide. The vest had been a shirt until Govil tore off the long sleeves. They had been included in a basket of things that had been confiscated when she was captured. Ganon had sent Shemei to get it after her bath. In the basket were also a bandoleer containing six throwing knives, a belt, a dagger in a sheath, a pair of thick-soled traveling boots, and a pair of throwing knives in forearm-mounted sheaths. The guards agreed not to reattach the chains as long as Anna did not attempt to escape. They ordered that she was to be barefoot unless they needed to travel on foot. And, of course, they refused to let her have any weapons.

"What are we waiting for?" Govil asked in irritation. "The queen commanded that we kill Gho-Bazh and bring back Deb-Roh."

"To begin with," Anna said, "I have not eaten in who knows how long. Shemei will return with food shortly. We will depart after we eat. "

"What do you suggest we need for this journey?" Lamb asked, trying to break the tension. Govil scowled, but Ganon knew what he was doing and unrolled a rough map.

"Assuming Gho-Bazh is at his palace in Kreipsche," he pointed to a castle symbol, "we will cross the Narrows." He referred to an isthmus that connected the so-called Isle of Brynne to the surrounding continent. "From there, we will skirt the Endless Barrens of None," indicating a mountainous region dominated by a large plateau, "down the Tiornen road. We will probably need to resupply in Tiornen," a city symbol, "before heading up the Weltschmerz road along the eastern side of the Groaning Slopes of Woe." The indicated road passed between a mountain range to the west and the plateau to the east.

"That's the easy part," Ganon continued. "Once we reach the Dirge, Gho-Bazh's troops will be patrolling the area and we'll have to sneak past them, around the mountains to Kreipsche, and then into his palace."

"How long will that take?" Anna asked.

"If things are favorable," Govil said, "we should be in Kreipsche before the snows fall there."

"About four cycles of the moon," Ganon replied.

Chapter 9

Dhath Gl'clot 11

The city outside the palace was a maze of whitewashed adobe. The streets were crowded with merchants, shoppers, and others, all human and carefully watched by insect-man guards with mancatchers. As she scanned the scene, Anna noted that there were no apparent archers.

She and Lamb waited with Ganon while Govil negotiated with a merchant for large, reptilian beasts of burden. Some had long, scythe-like claws extending from the front pair of their six legs. The others had three pairs of legs that ended in five-clawed toes.

"While we wait here," Anna said to Ganon, "tell me who you think I am."

"You are Nygof of Kreipsche," the guard replied. "You are said to be a spy and assassin, and an expert with knives thrown and in hand."

"And what of my reputation?" Anna probed.

"You are not known to use poison or kill by ambush," Ganon continued. "It is said that you always confront victims and tell them why before you kill them."

"And why am I the Queen's prisoner?"

"You came to Brynner to assassinate the Queen for Gho-Bazh. You used your underworld contacts to sneak into the city, and Deb-Roh's magic to enter the palace."

"And you captured me?"

"No, you were already in the cells before Govil and I were assigned to guard you."

"So everything you know about her is hearsay?" Lamb asked. Ganon looked hesitant. "You don't have any first-hand knowledge of who she is or what she has done."

"I have my instructions from the Queen," Ganon said, snapping his mandibles, "and that is all that I need."

◆

"All the guards are blurry too," O'Malley asked, squinting through tired eyes at the monochrome image. "Why are they concealed from Harry?"

"The Junazhi believe that the concealed beings are of an insectoid origin. Their other senses detect such characteristics."

"And they are trying to buy those six-legged reptiles as transportation. This is all in Brian Teplow's imagination?"

"The world we are viewing is the creation of Brian Teplow's mind."

◆

"I have acquired six shufflers; two males and four females," Govil announced when the group came at his summons.

"Ganon and I will ride the males. You two and the gear will be carried on the females." He looked to Anna and Lamb. "Should we lose one, we can transfer the gear to your mounts."

The wrangler led them to the six skinny creatures. One of them approached Anna, and puffed a cloud of moist air over her face before sucking it back in again. Then the shuffler stood by her side. Anna took the reins.

"She seems to like you," Govil said with a scowl. "It is said that Nygof is a friend to all beasts." He glanced at the shackles which were visible in a pouch on his harness, but then just walked past and took the reins of one of the armed mounts.

"They're not the best specimens," Ganon said after glancing at the six, "but they will have to do. We'll just need to keep the gear to a minimum."

Lamb selected another of the females. It screeched at him. He approached slowly and allowed the shuffler to examine him, which it did front and back with its long neck. Then it exhaled and inhaled on him, and stood its ground. Lamb took the reins, and the beast grunted.

"Hold the reins of the other two," Ganon said, leading the other male shuffler. He watched as Lamb and Anna each approached the remaining creatures, who inspected them before allowing them to lead them on.

◆

The blazing red sun was high in a cloudless, purple sky when the expedition passed through the North Gate. They had acquired a large number of water skins. Each of the mounts carried four, and one of the pack beasts bore three large casks. They had purchased soft, flat loaves that they rolled up and stuffed in their saddle bags. They piled trade goods on the other shuffler.

Govil led the way, followed by Lamb, then Anna, and finally Ganon. Lamb and Anna each had a pack animal tethered to their mount.

The countryside around the city of Brynner was green and lush with large-leaved bushes and towering trees. The road was packed earth, and Anna watched as the sides of the path were cleared by slaves overseen by insect-men. She was about to ask why when she heard a scream and looked to watch the feet of a man disappear into the maw of a giant, carnivorous plant.

"Everything here is dangerous," Govil shouted back to Lamb. "Do not approach anything and only go where I tell you to."

"What do you mean by everything?"

"The bushes bite, the trees have poisonous bark and acidic fruits and the grass can be razor sharp. The shufflers are protected by thick hides, but you should not stray from the path."

Lamb gulped and nodded his understanding, though Govil was not looking at him.

"How far will we travel today?" Anna shouted to Ganon behind her.

"If we can reach the Narrows at low tide, we will cross and camp on the other side. If not, we will camp on this side of the Narrows and cross wait. There is a clearing there for just that purpose."

"Why wait?"

"Because the inhabitants of the twin lakes pull travelers into the depths when the tide is high, and they can reach across the Narrows."

◆

"What in the name of all that is holy is that?!" O'Malley cried as the faces became more distinct.

As he watched, the blurry outlines of their heads became insect-like, with bulbous, compound eyes, pointed beaks, and sharply pointed mandibles.

"The Junazhi say that the illusion has faded. That is how they actually appear."

"I've never heard of anything like that," O'Malley said. In all his studies of ancient history and mythology, he had never come across insect-beings.

◆

Lamb did not realize that Govil and Ganon's true features had been revealed until he noticed the guards at the Narrows. At the top of a small rise, they looked over the narrow strip of land that separated the twin lakes, Aeryne and Feryne, and connected the Isle of Brynn to the landmass beyond that stretched featurelessly as far as the eye could see.

Lamb noticed a handful of guards posted at the near end and that was when he saw the mandibles, and then the compound eyes. He turned to his companions to say something, and saw that Anna was not surprised that their escorts also had insect heads.

The sun was setting over the mountains in the distance. As they watched, the isthmus visibly narrowed with the arrival of each wave.

"Quickly now," Govil shouted, coaxing his mount to run, "we must cross before the tide comes in. Otherwise we have to cross in the early morning, when it will be dark."

Lamb kicked the shuffler's flanks, but the beast did not respond. Anna pulled her reins back, as if to stop a horse, and her mount took off, with the pack animal running behind her. Lamb pulled back on his reins, and his shuffler quickly caught up to and passed Anna's.

With each length, the waters grew steadily closer. Lamb noticed movement beneath the rapidly approaching surface on both sides. Suddenly, a tentacle lashed out toward him, but fell short. More tentacles groped at them from both sides, growing steadily closer.

Lamb saw that Govil had reached the other side of the Narrows, and the guard turned back. Then the insect man jerked the reins and the shuffler bounded back toward them.

At the same time, a tentacle wrapped around one of the legs of Anna's beast. The creature stumbled, but righted itself when Ganon's mount sliced through it and then several others with its scythe-like forelimbs.

Govil took up a position on the other side and had his mount slash at the tentacles there.

When they reached the opposite bank, the Narrows were less than a shuffler-length wide. The tentacles groped along the surface and fought over the severed ends of their peers.

The group stopped by squeezing their legs on the chests of their mounts and then all dismounted.

"Inspect your beast," Govil said with authority. "See that there are no wounds." He then pulled an animal skin from a saddlebag and wiped the gore from his mount's forelegs and chest. Ganon did the same with practiced ease.

Anna looked carefully at the leg that had been seized by the tentacle. There was a rough patch where it looked like some scales had been scraped off, but there was no signed of a laceration. She checked out the rest of the creature, which stood calmly for her inspection. Then she looked over the pack lizard.

Lamb tried to follow suit, but his mount turned her neck or body to keep him in view. The animal had not been hit by anything, and did not seem to be injured. Anna joined him a moment later after examining Lamb's pack animal.

"She looks to be in good condition," she said.

"Let's get moving," Govil said from his saddle. "We want to be in the foothills before dark."

◆

"That is a strange place," O'Malley said after watching the narrow escape across the isthmus.

"According to Sigmund Freud," Bierce said, "the imagery of the mind is representative of repressed desires."

"And what do insect-men and tentacled monsters symbolize?"

"The Junazhi hypothesize that the world we are viewing is a corrupted union of Teplow's and Kovacs' thoughts."

"I hope Anna and Harry can separate the two."

◆

The caravan had climbed up a slope from the shore and through a gap in a low stone wall. Beyond the wall, Anna saw a vast plateau rise farther on the opposite side of a wide, well-traveled path that wound in both directions around the twin lakes on either side of the Narrows. A large, flat section of the stone face across from the gap in the wall was inscribed with strange characters that Anna could somehow discern by the fading light of the setting sun. The sign indicated that Tiornen was to the left, and Len Lorche was to the right.

"We will camp here," Govil said as he tethered his shuffler to one of several stone rings on either side of the sign. As Anna dismounted, she was caught by Ganon, who promptly snapped the chains to her wrist and leg cuffs, expertly passed the connecting chain from her ankles through one of the rings and to Anna's wrists.

"We had an agreement," Lamb cried as he attempted to pull Anna away from the guard. Ganon kicked him in the chest and the doctor fell to the ground.

"I agreed not to try to escape," Anna said angrily, "I agreed not to wear shoes, and I agreed to be unarmed. Why have you bound me again?"

"Your word is yet to be proven," Govil said scornfully. "We will not face the Queen's wrath should you escape us."

"But she'll be completely vulnerable like this," Lamb replied. "What if some fearsome beasts attack us in the night?!"

"We will also not fail in our mission," Ganon said. "We will ensure that both of you survive to complete the Queen's commands."

"Be content that we do not strip you," Govil added. "Your reputation for improvisational weaponry is known to us."

"And who will protect her from *you*?" Lamb asked pointedly.

"You are welcome to try," Govil replied.

Chapter 10

Dhath Gl'clot 11

Anna stood facing the rock wall that sloped up from the twin lakes. It was cold, dry, and dark, unlike the bright, hot, and humid afternoon, though she could tell that the moon was rising beyond the lip of the plateau before her. She was tethered in the center of the six shufflers between the two pack animals. The beasts she and Lamb had ridden were next, while the scythe-armed males were tied up on the outside.

The ring was set just above her waist level, and she had had to stand on her toes until Lamb piled some large, flat stones to raise her up. Anna was tired too. Her legs ached and her bare feet against the cold stone gave her chills, which a light breeze along the road amplified periodically.

Anna and Lamb had protested at length until Ganon clamped his mandibles lightly onto Lamb skull. Govil then gagged Anna with a leather bit that was only removed when

Lamb had persuaded Govil to let him hand feed her from the ration packet that the guard deigned to allow her to eat. Anna could tell that the abrasive guard was just being obstinate, but they were armed, Lamb was not, and she was shackled. Their hostility toward her was evident. Ganon seemed to be better able to control his temper, but he clearly deferred to Govil.

While Anna ate, the human pair considered their situation.

"This is not the vision of Brian Teplow," Anna said. "We were allied. You, me, Ganon, Govil, and Sif were on the expedition to rescue Brian together. Now, Brian, or rather Deb-Roh, and Gho-Bazh are allied, and we are Sif's prisoners."

"Liv was clearly hostile toward you," Lamb replied, smiling at the memory of her costume, "but I could tell that she was still smitten with me."

"Liv is gone!" Anna whispered with irritation. "She was transformed by Utgarda's touch into that slug-witch. Did you not see that trail of larvae appearing from behind her?"

"What are you talking about?" Lamb looked confused. "She was the same as when we met her at her apartment."

"You are telling me that Sif looked perfectly normal to you?" Anna said in frustration.

"Yes."

"That everyone in the throne room was human?"

"Of course."

"And what of Ganon and Govil?" Anna said, tilting her head toward where Ganon stood watch. She noted a glimmer of understanding in Lamb's expression. "She must have cast some kind of spell on you, and we have passed beyond its range of effect." Lamb turned pale.

"Now you can see Sif's minions for what they really are. Those insect people are her *offspring*! Sif is a hive queen! An insect! Ganon and Govil are her soldiers. Like ants! And, like ants, they are devoted to and live only to serve their queen."

"I must admit," Lamb said with a sigh, "that as absurd as that sounds, it seems to be the case. If this is a world of Brian's imagination, anything is possible." He paused. "But why have you been cast as an assassin?"

"Sif said she knew who I was in the throne room. For some reason, she blames me for her transformation."

"We went to the Church of Cosmic Understanding to find you. She insisted on scouting ahead and ended up in that sacrificial pit." He gave Anna a despairing look. "If we hadn't been looking for you… if I hadn't been so worried about you…"

Anna peered into his eyes. They were moist with unshed tears. She unconsciously tried to raise her hands to wipe them away, but the chains stopped her.

"I know," she said softly. "I would have done the same for you."

Lamb wrapped his arms around Anna and sobbed quietly on her shoulder until he was abruptly pulled away by Ganon and effortlessly tossed to the other side of the road.

"Stay there or I will bind you as well," Anna heard the guard say. Then her head was pulled back by the hair.

"If you conspire to impede or prevent our mission," Govil said, his mandibles gently pinching at her temples, "you will be fully bound and have to walk to Kreipsche." He released her head and hair. "Now be quiet or you will attract the creatures of the night."

◆

Anna was awakened by a strong arm grabbing her waist from behind and a hand covering her mouth. She had sunk to a seated position, her arms thrust above her head by the chains. As she was lifted to her feet, another humanoid form started working at the chain that passed through the stone ring. It was a man, and he quietly inspected the length of the chains from Anna's wrists to her ankles. She heard furtive movement behind her as well.

Suddenly, the grip on Anna tightened momentarily and then a man's head bounced off the stones Anna had been sitting on and out of sight, followed by the headless body, which sprayed the man at Anna's feet with blood. Before Anna could react, the second man was spitted through the chest by the spear end of Ganon's mancatcher. Anna heard a brief commotion behind her as well before all turned silent again, save for the sound of gurgling.

"Friends of yours?" Ganon asked, staring into the impaled man's horrified face.

Anna shook her head. The man was dressed in garments similar to Anna's. Blood trickled from his mouth and he tried to speak, all the while his eyes darted back and forth between Anna and Ganon. Anna stared back, unable to speak herself.

"How about this one?" he said when he returned with the severed head a moment later.

"I do not know who these people are," Anna replied.

"Good," Ganon said. Then he punctured the skull with his mandibles and pierced it with his beak. There was the slurping sound, and then Ganon tilted his head back and swallowed. "Delicious," he said after dropping the empty skull. The man on the ground started burbling anew. Ganon raised the man to a sitting position, and then fed on the contents of his skull as the man stared with horror at Anna.

◆

"Good lord!" O'Malley cried as he watched one of the insect man empty a man's skull.

"They ingest their food like insects. They liquefy the contents and then drink it," Bierce advised. "However, they do seem to be intent on protecting Dr. Rykov from harm."

"A lot of good that will do if assailants can easily sneak up and overpower her."

◆

"I was completely at their mercy like this," she fumed as Ganon released the dead man. "I could have been killed, and then you would have failed your Queen!"

"Even so," Govil said from behind her, "better that way than the alternative."

He turned her head to its limit so Anna could see a line of people chained together. Some were gagged while others whimpered quietly. They were all dressed in simple furs and tanned leather, and all were barefoot. They were linked together by metal collars around their necks, while their wrists and ankles were shackled like her own.

"They would have added you to the line and moved on," he said with a grimace, "probably back to Brynner." He chuckled as he released her head. "They would have been in for a surprise when the Queen saw you!"

"Nevertheless," Lamb said awkwardly, stumbling toward Anna, "she could not defend herself or even flee from them. If their intent had been murder, she would be dead now!" He stood before Anna and put his hands on her shoulders. "Are you all right?"

"I am fine," Anna said tersely, eyeing Govil. "They did not have a chance to do anything."

"Precisely," Govil said. "We are only here to see that both of you complete your tasks for the Queen. We will protect you."

"And what about when we get to Kreipsche? What is to stop me from turning on you then? Or do you intend to have me kill Gho-Bazh while still in chains." She glared at Govil.

"We need to complete this mission for our own reasons," Lamb said.

"And we would have pursued it even without the Queen's interference."

Suddenly, Govil and Ganon stood motionless. Anna glanced from one to the other, but they did not move until Lamb waved his hand in front of Ganon's face. In a flash, the guard grabbed the doctor's hand and wrenched his arm behind his back, but was otherwise motionless. Then they both seemed to reanimate. Ganon released Lamb's arm, while Govil produced the three small keys from his armguard and removed the chains from Anna's cuffs.

"We will allow you to remain at liberty," Ganon said, "but do not abuse our generosity."

"You will sleep over there," Govil said, pointing across the path to where Lamb had been. Lamb followed Anna to the indicated place. She stretched her sore arms and attempted to rub her wrists under the irons. Govil and Ganon resumed their positions to scan the path in each direction.

"What about them?" Lamb asked, indicating the coffle of prisoners as Govil walked past. The guard stopped to examine each in turn, pulling their heads back by the hair to look in their mouths. Looking over their bodies. Touching them until each protested feebly. Eventually, he dragged the lead chain and tethered it to the ring that Anna had been occupying. Then he pushed the woman at the front of the line in the chest. She fell backward into the woman behind her and the line toppled like dominoes until all were seated. Then he continued to his post.

Lamb rose to see to the women, but Govil and Ganon both turned with their weapons at the ready.

"Do not approach them," Ganon said.

"Do not talk to them," Govil warned. "Do not interact with them in any way." Then they both turned and resumed their watch.

◆

O'Malley sighed as Anna was released from confinement. Lamb followed her back to where he had been sleeping, but stopped and turned toward a line of people chained together by the neck. The guards both turned and appeared to threaten him. Lamb went over to Anna, laid down behind her on the ground, and wrapped an arm around her. Anna's eyes were already closed, but she snuggled up against him before the doctor closed his eyes.

Chapter 11

Dhath Gl'clot 11

Anna awoke on the ground with Lamb's arm wrapped around her. The warmth of his body had greatly eased the chills of her confinement, but now it was getting hot and humid again. She lifted his arm from around her waist and rose to a sitting position. Lamb stirred with the motion.

"Good morning," he said drowsily. He stood and stretched.

Anna rubbed at her wrists beneath the cuffs. They were starting to chafe, and purple rings were peaked out from beneath the thick two-inch bands. Then she leaned forward. The cuffs clinked with her leg iron as she touched her toes. At the sound, she noticed Govil watching her from where he stood next to his mount. She scowled at him, and his beak snapped open and closed a few times in response, but he did not say anything. Her ankles were also bruised.

"Let me take a look at those," Lamb said, taking Anna's wrists in his hands. "We need to get these cuffs off." He examined the metal bands and noticed that there were no seams. They each appeared to be one piece of metal precisely fitted to her. "They're going to have to be cut off."

"I do not think our friends will approve of that," Anna said. Lamb looked around and found the thin cloth wrapping of the rations they had consumed. He tore it into wide strips and gently slid one under each of the cuffs. Anna winced, but didn't cry out.

"That should ease the chafing at least."

"Thank you, Harry." She kissed his cheek.

"Let's get going," Ganon shouted. The sky beyond the lip of the rise was turning from purple to red. Ganon and Govil were readying their mounts. The other shufflers were still tethered to the rings. There was no sign of the chained people.

"What happened to the prisoners?" Lamb asked.

"They have been dealt with," Govil replied dismissively. "None of your concern. Now ready your beasts. We depart when the sun hits the rise."

"We need to eat and prepare ourselves," Lamb replied.

"Then you shouldn't have slept so long," Ganon said. "You can eat on the road."

"Where are you going?" Govil shouted.

"I need to relieve myself," Anna replied from the gap in the wall that led to the Narrows.

"You will not leave our sight," the guard commanded. "Whatever you need, you can attend to it in our presence."

"It is nothing we haven't seen before," Ganon added. Anna glared at them and pulled down her trousers where she stood. Lamb turned away and readied the four shufflers. When he turned back, Anna was at his side. She took the reins of her mount and climbed onto the shuffler's back.

Lamb handed Anna a ration bundle from his saddle bag, took one for himself, and then mounted his own shuffler. Then the column moved forward in silence.

◆

The path wound around the side of the rise following the shoreline of Aeyrne, the western of the twin lakes, for several days. The terrain grew increasingly more bleak and featureless. They passed no other traffic.

Each night, as the sun set over the lake, they stopped at one of several sets of rings mounted in the wall roughly half a day's mounted travel apart. These were apparently designated camping places.

Initially, Lamb had attempted to make conversation, but the guards demanded that he be silent lest they be attacked by enemies or bandits lying in wait. Lamb found it strange that they were wary of attacks and yet camped at known campsites each night, but he knew better than to question the insect-men.

They had fallen into a routine where Govil would threaten to bind Anna if she or Lamb attempted to escape, and then he and Ganon went about tending to their mounts and taking up positions watching the path in each direction. Apparently, the insect-men did not sleep.

The low wall on the lake side rose and fell with the landscape, growing taller than Anna in places where the terrain dropped nearing the level of the lake shore. The rise on the other side of the path seemed to be of a constant height, and Anna realized that the plateau above had once been on the lake shore.

There were no other gaps in the lake-side wall, which appeared to be regularly maintained - unlike the road itself - which was merely packed dirt augmented by intermittent ruts and fissures, particularly in the low-lying sections of the path.

Anna noticed that Govil carefully examined the wider fissures before taking his shuffler across.

"What are you looking for?" she asked. Govil glared at her.

"Barrens leeches," he said without emotion. "They burrow under the earth and strike when the rains come and the ground is moist. Sometimes there is water just below the surface that they gather in. They will attack our mounts if we are not careful."

No leeches rose from the crevasses. They continued on in silence, stopping periodically where the path rose to survey to road ahead. The way was more or less straight, following the shore of the lake, until it rose one last time as Aeyrne curved away to the south.

◆

O'Malley woke abruptly. He was seated in a chair at the table. The Kovacs cylinder had been removed, and the Bierce device now sat to one side. He glanced about the room and noticed sunlight coming from the windows in the other room. A lantern was lit on the table before him, and Billy walked in carrying a tray bearing a plate of fried eggs, sausage links, biscuits, and a pot of coffee. O'Malley eyed the tray and its bearer suspiciously.

"**Good morning,**" Bierce said. "**Billy has brought you your favorite breakfast.**"

"How long was I asleep?"

"**Your body has been dormant for some time, but your mind was quite active during that time. I hope Billy has prepared the meal to your liking. The Junazhi gave him specific instructions.**"

"They can read my mind?" O'Malley said in panic.

"**The Junazhi can detect your surface thoughts when your body is dormant. That is another reason why they** confine themselves to remote areas. The mental noise is overwhelming to them."

O'Malley was not reassured, but he managed to relax a little. He glanced at the meal. It looked and smelled delicious, but he was wary of the silent caretaker.

"Billy will not harm you," Bierce said. "He is the agent of the Junazhi. He takes care of the facilities and ensures that knowledge of the Junazhi is contained. While you are here, he will provide for your needs."

"Can you read my mind?" O'Malley said as he picked up the fork and knife. "You seem to know what I am thinking."

"Though I am now housed in this device, I had seventy-two years in my human shell. I can surmise your wants and needs. I'm sure that you are concerned for the well-being of your friends." O'Malley glanced to where Anna and Lamb had been sitting, and noticed that their bodies had been laid down on a pile of rugs. "Billy made them more comfortable, and has been moving their limbs regularly to keep them from stiffening up."

"He seems to have had a lot of practice maintaining unconscious people," O'Malley mused. The food was indeed exactly how he liked it, down to the seasoning of the sausages and the buttermilk in the biscuits. "Does he do this often?"

"They are not unconscious. Their minds are elsewhere. Those physical shells merely function mechanically. They are otherwise inert." O'Malley spit out his meal in surprise.

"What do you mean their minds are elsewhere?"

"The Junazhi extracted their minds and facilitated transport to the other realm. They now exist there, not here."

"So, what they are experiencing there isn't a dream. It's real!"

"Precisely. They are there, and whatever they experience in that place is actually happening to them."

"So if they are harmed, the injuries will persist on their return?"

"I have not experienced this kind of out-of-body travel before. When the brains are preserved in the cylinders, any physical needs are maintained by the device, and the physical residue is discarded. Their bodies, however, lay dormant and subject to Billy's ministrations."

O'Malley's appetite was waning, and he ate little of the excellent meal. He watched Billy bend Lamb's arms and legs a few times, turn his head, and sit him up and lay him down again. O'Malley ate absently, watching the exercises, which were conducted gently and with care.

When Billy moved on to Anna, the father rose and went to her side. As Billy lifted her left arm, Anna's sleeve slipped up her arm revealing a bruised ring around her wrist. O'Malley examined her other arm and saw a similar bruise. Her arms were cold in spite of the long sleeves of her blouse and jacket. He pulled up her trouser legs and noted similar bruises around both ankles, though her legs were warmer than her arms. Anna's actual body was exhibiting the physical trauma that her mind had experienced. Her stomach gurgled as if in agreement.

O'Malley gave Lamb a similar examination. The doctor's body was also cooler, though not a cold as Anna's, but in the monitor, Lamb was fully clothed, while Anna had on only a vest and trousers.

"Get them some blankets," he said to Billy.

Chapter 12

Dhath Gl'clot 12

When Anna reached the summit, she gasped. The bleak plateau that stretched on infinitely was the same one she had seen for a moment in the New York Subway, as well as in Brian Teplow's sketchbook.

"The Endless Barrens of None," Govil said with resignation.

Mountains were barely visible in the distance to the north and west. The surface of the entire expanse was made of flat, featureless, reddish stone as far as the eye could see.

"Where do we go from here?" Lamb asked as he halted his shuffler alongside Anna's.

"Beyond those mountains lies the domain of Gho-Bazh," Ganon said ominously. His mount rounded on Lamb's, and the guard reined it in sharply. "Around the northernmost top is the city of Kreipsche."

"This road continues along the southern edge to Tiornen," Govil continued, "and then curves northward along the eastern foot of the Groaning Slopes of Woe. We will follow this path to Tiornen and, as long as we are not detected, we will continue into the foothills and overland parallel to it."

"Won't that route greatly increase our chance of discovery?" Lamb asked. "Why go to Tiornen at all? Why not avoid other travelers and go straight toward the mountains? That would surely be more secure."

"As the name suggests," Govil replied, "there is nothing between here and there aside from rock, heat, and death. There is no cover for the likes of you and I. Predators of all kinds will see us coming from far off and set upon us unawares if we venture from the trail."

"And you will need food and water by the time we reach Tiornen," Ganon added. "Ration your remaining supplies. There won't be anything edible until we descend off the Barrens again."

"You said we would continue on the road if we were not detected," Anna said. "Who would be looking for us? And happens if we are seen?" Govil eyed Anna suspiciously.

"If Gho-Bazh becomes aware of us," he said in irritation, "he will send his troops to rescue you." He clicked his mandibles savagely. "Know that I will kill you myself and feast on your brains before you are reunited with the sorcerer."

"If we lose the advantage of stealth," Ganon said, "we will have to circle around the Groaning Slopes of Woe and trek through the jungles of Folly to avoid pursuit. That would be better than attempting to cross the mountains themselves, but the jungle will be more difficult than the road around the Barrens."

"And once we clear Folly," Govil added, "the wild beast-men will be more savage than those who serve Gho-Bazh should we find ourselves overcome by them."

"Do you mean the Pointees?" Lamb asked. The guards looked uncertain. "Tall, hairy things with horns and hooves?"

"Those are the beast-men," Ganon said with a nod. "Gho-Bazh has tamed an army of them, but the wild ones in the hills between Folly and Kreipsche are a danger all their own."

"Your allegiance to Gho-Bazh will not save you from them," Govil said with a sneer. "They hate him as much as our Queen. They will pluck the marrow from your bones as well as ours."

◆

"I've seen that before," O'Malley cried as he rose from his seat and ran toward the shelf that held Anna's purse. Billy rose and blocked his path.

"Step aside," the priest commanded, but the silent watchman held his ground.

"**What are you doing?**" Bierce asked.

"Brian Teplow drew images of a similar journey. His sketchbook is in Anna's bag." O'Malley moved to go around, but Billy stepped in front of him again.

"Oh, come on!" O'Malley shouted. "If I wished to harm you, I would use this." He held up his left hand, still encased in the relic, pointing toward the ceiling.

Billy looked toward the Bierce device. A moment later he reached up to the shelf and retrieved the purse, holding it open for the priest. The big man watched warily as O'Malley removed the sketchbook. He placed it on the table and opened to the two-page spread of the barren, flat, rocky plain.

"**Please angle the book toward my visual receptors.**" O'Malley tilted the book. "**That does appear to match what Dr. Lamb is viewing. Does that document the entire journey?**"

"Yes and no," O'Malley replied. "It seems to parallel their experience, but there are differences. For starters, Anna is not a prisoner here," he pointed to the book absently. "And all the participants are friends in Teplow's account."

A Junazhi appeared next to O'Malley and peered at the image. It grasped the book in its second pair of limbs and flipped through the pages with one of its forelimbs while tapping various images with the tip of its other. The orbs on its head flashed hypnotically in conversation with Bierce and also with other Junazhi that O'Malley realized were present but not visible.

"The Junazhi hypothesize that the imagery of Brian Teplow has been altered by the influence of Kovacs. This is most unprecedented and the Junazhi are quite intrigued."

◆

Anna blinked as she gazed into the bleak landscape, which lay beneath an endless array of stars in a sea of purplish-black, despite the light pollution of the hot reddish sun that dominated the sky. They dismounted to water the shufflers and stretch their legs.

The heat haze rising from the stone floor in the distance blurred the faint outline of the mountains to the north. As Anna stared into the haze, an indistinct form gradually came into sharper focus. She gasped as she saw the three-legged giant with the enormous, red, elephantine trunk; Utgarda. Lamb heard the sound and looked to see, followed by Govil and Ganon. The scaly giant spread its palms toward them, making eye contact with Anna.

"The Lord of the Endless Barrens is sending you his greeting," Govil said ominously. "We must be on our guard lest his minions, the Draunskur, swarm and slay us."

"You do not have many friends," Anna said sarcastically, "do you?" Govil looked to her quizzically. "The Pointees will eat us. The Draunskur will just kill us. Gho-Bazh will destroy us all. And those are just the people that you have mentioned."

"The Pointees hate all who are not like them-" Govil started.

"But they serve Gho-Bazh," Lamb interrupted. "Is he a Pointee? I thought he was human."

"He is a sorcerer," Govil replied. "He is whatever he wishes to be. He has dominated the minds of some of the Pointees."

"We are safer with them than with the wild ones," Ganon said. "At least they will kill us before we're eaten." Lamb could not tell if the guard was joking. He glanced to Anna, but her gaze was fixed on Utgarda.

"Utgarda and Gho-Bazh are enemies, yes?" she asked. "And we are on our way to kill Gho-Bazh. If this is true, then why are we afraid of Utgarda?" Govil and Ganon glanced to each other, then Govil slapped Anna across the face and knocked her to the ground.

"Do not play mind games with us," the violent insect-man said. "The Lord of the Barrens is a friend to no one. He cares nothing of the likes of us. We cannot understand how he thinks or why he does what he does."

Anna rubbed her face as Lamb helped her to her feet. Ganon had the chains in his hands, but Lamb gently pushed them away. Lamb stared at the guard, who exchanged glances with Govil, and then returned them to his saddlebag.

"Where did he go?" Anna said, looking back toward the mountains. Utgarda was no longer there. "It was no mirage," she said in awe. "You all saw it."

"What we saw is that our mission has been marked," Govil spat. "Utgarda knows of our presence. Our stealth has been compromised."

"How does that impact our journey?" Lamb asked with concern in his voice.

"As you said," Govil replied, "Utgarda is at odds with Gho-Bazh. And he has no reason to consider us one way or another." He paused, considering, and then said, "We continue as planned until something causes us to revise our route. Mount up."

◆

As the hot sun blazed malevolently in the dark sea of stars, the terrain grew flatter. The ground seemed to smoke in places, and the travelers could feel the heat billowing up from below. The shufflers seemed unimpaired by the heat, and Lamb noticed that they now walked on their thick, extended claws rather than their feet, using the pointed tips to seek purchase in the crags and cracks of the stony ground.

The reddish light of the dominant star gave everything an orangey-pink hue, with the ground melting into the still-distant mountains that thrust up into the inky sky. The road they followed had left the lake behind several days prior, and was now barely visible in the uniform texture of the stone.

As before, Govil stifled any kind of conversation, stating that they were under constant surveillance in spite of the lack of any visible signs of life anywhere. There were no plants, animals, birds, or insects. The only sound was an occasional buzzing hum of the hot wind.

By day, Anna and Lamb sweat greatly, but drank sparingly as there had been no signs of water since they left the shores of Aeryne. By night, the temperatures plummeted, and Anna and Lamb slept together, both for bodily warmth and the sense of security. Their guards did not seem to need sleep, nor did they seem particularly affected by the varying temperatures.

The twilight hours, during which they rested the shufflers and the human ate their rations, were the only time conversation was allowed. They made no fire. There was nothing to burn, and they had brought nothing with them with which to make one. And once full dark fell, silence was again the rule.

"How far have we gone?" Lamb asked Ganon as he and Anna ate. "I don't see any way to gauge our progress."

"By my estimate, we are approximately one third of the way to Tiornen," he replied.

"What makes you think so?" Anna asked. "Do you navigate by the stars?"

"The stars are liars," Ganon replied. "They change to suit their own purposes." He pointed behind them. "Watch."

As she looked to the east, the sun set beyond the mountains behind her, and Anna saw more and more stars blink into existence as if switches were being flipped. They appeared at random. Some nearer. Some farther away. Some brighter than others. Then, just as suddenly as they had winked on, random stars disappeared, while others visibly moved around in the sky.

"Amazing," Lamb said in awe. "There doesn't seem to be any pattern to their movements. Obviously, they would be useless for navigation, so how do you know where you are going?"

"We listen," the guard replied.

"Listen to what?" Anna asked.

"We listen to the stones beneath us as they grind together. And we listen to the echo of the mountains and the sound of the wind. They tell us where we are and where we are going."

They sat in silence for a few moments while Anna and Lamb tried to hear what the insect-men did, but they could not. Perhaps the sounds were beyond the range of human perception.

"I don't hear anything," Lamb said with frustration. "But as long as you know where we are going, we should make it."

𝖟

Chapter 13

July 16, 1929

    O'Malley's eyes were bloodshot and his head spun with fatigue. He had nodded off again. During his previous lapse, a week had apparently passed for Anna and Harry. Now, when he looked at the image in the alien device, the scene had changed yet again. The landscape was without features and in a uniform grayish color. Harry and Anna were clearly under-nourished, and both looked hot and weak.

    Billy returned bearing the tray of hot tea and freshly baked muffins with an assortment of jams and butter. When did Billy find the time to make these meals? Then again, the Junazhi existed outside of time, apparently, so maybe Billy was able to benefit from their influence.

"You need to attend to your physical needs better, Father. I assure you that I will not let you miss anything important. There is nothing you can do to assist them."

"How long was I asleep?" O'Malley asked absently. They had already established that Bierce had no reference for the passage of time, and the uncommunicative Billy functioned almost mechanically. "Rather, what has happened?"

"They have trekked many days through that barren wasteland without contact with anything or anyone. They appear to be well and in good spirits, given the circumstances."

O'Malley rose from his seat and stretched. Then he went to Anna's side and felt the pulse in her neck. She was still unconscious, breathing shallowly, and her skin was slightly cooler than normal in spite of the blankets that now covered her. When he removed her arm from beneath the covers. O'Malley noticed that the bruises around her wrists were less irritated, and that her skin was getting darker and dryer, reacting to that alien sun.

The father examined Lamb and noticed the same effects on him. He was indeed tanned and dry, but his body was cooler than normal, especially for one that was reacting to desert conditions. Nevertheless, O'Malley restored the covers and wiped their faces with a damp cloth for no reason other than it made him feel like he was doing something useful.

"I'm going outside for some air," O'Malley said as he rose. "I expect that nothing will have changed when I return."

"Do not attempt to leave," Bierce warned. "The Junazhi suffer your presence because they have no choice, but they will not allow you to expose them."

"There is no way I will abandon my friends to these monsters," O'Malley said with conviction. "I will return in a few minutes." He glared at Billy, who stood by the shelf containing their belongings, and proceeded through the outer room, up the stairs, and out the front door.

It was night, and the ever-present fog remained low to the ground. O'Malley took deep breaths of the warm, moist air. Through small gaps in the canopy high above, he could see stars. He noted how different the sky was above his friends. The celestial bodies above him remained fixed and constant. After a few minutes, he sighed and returned to the basement.

◆

It was mid-afternoon of the next day when Anna was tugged out of her shuffler from behind. She had tied the reins of her pack animal about her waist for convenience. The creature had followed compliantly for several days, so she secured them to herself to free her hands. Through them, Anna could sense when the pack animal was tired or alarmed. This time, however, something had surprised the shuffler, overpowered it, and stopped its forward movement, because Anna was yanked from her seat as her own mount continued forward.

Lamb saw a mass of tentacles burst from the solid stone of the path and wrap around the shuffler in from of him. The beast was pulled off its feet and slammed against the stone beneath it several times. The reins of the helpless creature went taut, and when they snapped back, Anna flew backward into the melee. As the flailing shuffler was slammed back and forth by its subterranean attacker, Anna flew through the air and hit the ground several times before the reins finally broke. She landed with a thud and lay motionless on her back.

"Protect the supplies," Ganon shouted to Lamb as he directed his mount to attack the tentacles with its scythe-like claws. Govil did the same. Lamb steered his mount and pack animal toward Anna and slid to the ground at her side. Anna was unconscious and bleeding from numerous cuts and abrasions, but the doctor saw no signs of other injury.

Lamb opened Anna's eyes, and her pupils reacted to the light. He examined her head and pressed gently against her neck, but detected no trauma. He felt up and down her arms and legs, but there were no signs of broken bones. Putting his ear to her mouth, he listened to her breathing. It was labored, and there was a slight wheeze.

Mechanically, Lamb unfastened Anna's vest, exposing her bare chest. A purpling bruise suggested fractured ribs. As he pressed gently against the unbruised ribs, Anna jumped, coughing and then wincing in pain. Lamb noted that there was no blood.

"Lay still," Lamb said calmly, "I think you have some cracked ribs, though I don't think you have punctured a lung. Do you feel any pain other than your ribs?"

"I feel sore everywhere," Anna replied. "But I do not think I have any other internal injuries."

"Can you feel your feet and your hands?" Anna moved her feet up and down, left and right, and then did the same with her hands and arms. "Good. Now try to sit up." Anna started to rise with Lamb's help, but quickly returned to the ground, covering the bruise with her hand.

"We need to get moving," Govil said as his shadow fell over Anna. "Your mating rituals can wait."

"She is injured and should not be moved," Lamb said with authority.

"You are to kill Gho-Bazh," Govil said to Anna. "I will not leave you to that creature when it has finished its current meal. As it is, we will have to divide the supplies we managed to salvage among the surviving mounts." He examined Anna's bruised chest impassively. "Rest here while we arrange things. Then we must get moving." He motioned to Lamb. "You come with me."

◆

Anna lay atop three crates that were lashed to the back of her shuffler. The tack that held them in place was also tied loosely around her waist and hips to keep her from falling off, and Lamb had covered her eyes with a damp cloth to shield them from the sun. In spite of the precautions, the movement of the boxes with the shuffler's gait pained her with each step.

It was the best Lamb could do. With no bandages or spare cloth to wrap around her, the doctor was reduced to tying ropes tightly over Anna's vest. Her breathing was normal, and she had not coughed up any blood, so he was confident that there had been no injury to her lungs. But Anna's ribs would take a very long time to heal. It was unlikely that she would be fit enough by the time they reached Kreipsche.

The caravan continued forward, slowly but steadily. Govil continued to lead, while Lamb held the reins to Anna's mount, and Ganon pulled the lone remaining pack animal. All the shufflers were overloaded, but their consumption of supplies along the way meant that the loss of the other pack animal had not been a hardship. However, they had lost half of their rations and, more importantly, more than half of their remaining water.

As always, Govil and Ganon seemed unaffected by the harsh environment. With Anna tied down, the insect-men had relaxed their guard on her. They did not see Lamb as a threat. But in light of Anna's injuries, and the even more meager rations that Govil now allowed, Lamb was pretty sure that the water would run out before they reached Tiornen.

Suddenly, Govil stopped the train with a gesture. He and Ganon froze in place. Lamb looked and listened, trying to detect whatever the guards were reacting to. He saw and heard nothing at first, but then he noted three small things in the distance, flying toward them at great speed.

A moment later, he felt a slight shaking of the ground. Then the guards quickly dismounted and Ganon motioned for Lamb to do the same. The doctor slid from his beast and ran for Anna, but tripped when Ganon grabbed his ankle with his mancatcher and pulled him back away from the shufflers. The two male shufflers were agitated, and circled the three females. They slashed their foreclaws menacingly in the air.

The flying creatures were upon them in the blink of an eye. There was something about them that was familiar to Lamb. They had scaly skin that blended into the dark sky underneath and the monochrome landscape on top. Humanoid faces were surmounted by writhing tentacles where the mouth and nose should have been. Large, pointed ears, bat-like wings, and talons sprouted from their feet. The flyers swooped and taunted the male shufflers, who sliced ineffectively at the attackers and circling the females defensively.

Lamb was horrified by the display, watching helplessly as Anna lay motionless, tied down in the midst of the fight. The guards were alert. Ganon released Lamb's ankle and twirled the weapon into position just before a dozen or more plumes of dust erupted from the ground all around them.

Small, degenerate people with pointed ears appeared as the clouds blew away. They had rough skin with the same coloring as the flyers, large eyes, large ears, with the appearance of emaciation. Lamb noted that the insect-men took them seriously. They had risen, and stood almost twice as tall as the small humanoids. They stood facing the crowd that had encircled them, moving in unison in a circular motion around the prone doctor.

There was a piercing shriek. Lamb followed the sound to see one of the flying creatures impaled on a shuffler claw. It was quickly rent in two by the beast's other claw, but with the defender's weapons occupied, the other two dove in and hacked at it with their talons, ripping large chunks of flesh from the creature each time.

At the same time, the small humanoids swarmed the insect-men. Ganon was pressed back and tripped over Lamb. The insect-man landed on his back and was hacked to pieces. Lamb covered his head with his arms and waited for the end.

But it didn't come. A moment later, the sounds of battle died down, and Lamb heard chittering conversation from the newcomers. Lamb looked up, and saw that pieces of Ganon had been scattered over a wide area.

Govil was on the ground in several large sections, his legs and lower abdomen separated from his torso. He threatened his attackers feebly with the claw end of his mancatcher. Several of the small combatants lay motionless in two or more cleanly sliced pieces around him. As he watched, Lamb saw three of the small humanoids carry Ganon's weapon over behind Govil. The others distracted him, and the three positioned the claw and snipped off the guard's head in a single, deft motion.

Lamb turned to the shufflers. The male animals had both been slain, and one of the flyers was eating from a carcass. Some of the small humanoids were taking the reins of the female creatures. Then he saw the other surviving flyer perched over Anna who lay motionless.

Lamb leapt into action and scrambled the short distance, yelling and waving his arms. A moment later, he climbed up onto Anna's mount and found the flyer rubbing its tentacled face on her chest leaving behind some kind of mucus. Lamb swatted at the creature with his hands ineffectually until the flyer beat its wings and pushed him off the shuffler's back. He landed hard and everything went black.

Chapter 14

?

Anna was moving through the darkness. She was in some kind of net, on her back with her arms at her sides, being pulled head first through soft, cool earth. Her body was sore all over, but she could feel moisture being absorbed through her skin. The darkness was close and confining, but she was unnaturally comfortable and at ease.

She did not know how long she had been unconscious. The last thing she remembered was the shufflers and the flying creatures fighting all around her. The flyers had resembled the form the cultists had taken when Utgarda appeared at the Church of Cosmic Understanding, and Anna realized that they had been partially transformed into the same flying beasts.

Anna tensed as she realized that they had been attacked and captured by Utgarda's minions, but she was unable to retain the distress. The comfort and solace the earth provided as her body flowed through it was overwhelming.

◆

"What the devil happened?" O'Malley cried as he reentered the basement chamber. He ran to the prone bodies of his friends. Anna's face was pale, and she groaned intermittently hugging her chest. O'Malley gently moved her hands aside, removed the blanket, and opened her jacket and blouse. She was covered with small cuts and abrasions, and there were several large bruises on her right side suggesting fractured ribs.

"They were attacked by some subterranean creature and Dr. Rykov was caught in the melee," Bierce said in his neutral, expressionless tone. **"Then they were attacked by some other people and subdued."**

"Help me," the priest said to Billy, who watched over his shoulder, as he gently sat Anna up to remove her jacket and blouse. A moment later, the watchman kneeled down and held her under the arms while O'Malley pulled the garments from her sleeves. Her arms and back were also cut and bruised.

"Get me my valise," he said absently to Billy. When nothing happened, he shouted, "NOW!" A moment later, Billy held the valise open so that he could see what the priest took from it. O'Malley rummaged through and removed a vial of green fluid and a roll of gauze. Billy grabbed the wrist holding the vial, but O'Malley yanked it free, removed the stopper, and poured the contents into the roll of gauze. He then rubbed it on Anna's cuts and bruises. There was a hissing sound as the fluid made contact with the wounds, and an acrid smell filled the air, but then the flesh of her many cuts and scrapes smoothed over and all but disappeared.

The ointment had no effect on the bruises beneath the skin, however, so O'Malley wrapped the fluid-soaked gauze tightly around her ribs, covering the bruises, and tied it as tightly as he could.

"That will have to do," he said with resignation, "until Harry can get a good look at her."

"Dr. Lamb is also in some distress," Bierce said.

O'Malley examined the doctor's unconscious form and noted a bleeding wound on the back of his head. Under Billy's watchful gaze, he reached into the valise and removed his last roll of gauze. He pressed the roll against the gauze around Anna to absorb some of the excess green fluid, and then gently wiped Lamb's head. It was superficial. Wadding up the wettest portion, he pressed it to the wound and wrapped the remainder of the roll around Lamb's head to hold it in place.

"The Junazhi wish to know if they are still functional," Bierce said. O'Malley glared at the canister since he could not see any of the aliens at the moment.

"If you mean are they still alive," he snarled, "then yes, they are still functional. The doctor's injury is minor, but Anna probably has several broken ribs. I doubt she will be of much use for this errand now."

Bierce's lights flashed and a Junazhi appeared at O'Malley's side. The being was transparent, and its forelimbs flitted about inside Anna's chest amidst her bruises. Within a few moments, the bruises faded to mere discolorations. Then the alien faded away again.

"The wounds to her shell should mend properly now," Bierce said, "but the Junazhi do not know what impact it will have on her mental form."

◆

Lamb awakened in a cave. The small, large-eyed, large-eared beings were all around. Their eyes glowed in the dim light. Several of the flying creatures entered through a hole a short distance away. Lamb was in a sitting position against the side of the cave, and felt unusually calm and well rested. He was not restrained in any way, but his clothing was torn to shreds, and he was covered from head to toe with dirt. As he slowly gathered his bearings, Anna walked up to him with a broad smile.

"Good morning," she said cheerily. "How do you feel?"

"Anna!" Lamb cried. "You're OK."

"I am whole and well," she said. "The Draunskur have rescued us, healed our injuries, and revitalized our bodies." Lamb realized that he was neither hungry nor thirsty anymore. "Apparently, while the surface of the Endless Barrens is dead, there are ample life energies beneath it, and we have absorbed enough to restore us back to good health."

"I'll say," Lamb said. "I haven't felt this good in years." He paused in the middle of his revelry. "How did you figure all this out?"

We spoke with her, a voice said in Lamb's head.

"They communicate telepathically," Anna said. "They don't have mouths."

"What do they want with us?" Lamb asked Anna. "What do you want with us?" he then said to the Draunskur gathered around them.

Our master wants you to complete your mission, the voice said. *And will help you.*

"The Draunskur are going to take us to the other side of the Endless Barrens, near Gho-Bazh's territory. It will save us weeks."

"What about guides and supplies?" Lamb asked. "We don't know where we are going."

We cannot go beyond the realm of our master. We will transport you as far as we are allowed.

"They have offered us equipment from the extensive collection of things they have acquired," Anna said.

She held out an ornate short sword for Lamb to inspect, and the doctor noticed that Anna was now dressed in sturdy traveling clothes under a thick coat of animal hide. In addition to the baldric for the sword she now held, Anna also had a bandoleer of thin knives over her shoulder, and tall leather boots on her feet.

"If you are ready," Anna said, pulling Lamb to his feet, "you can take your pick and we can be on our way."

◆

Some time later, Harry Lamb emerged from the burrow they had been sheltered in. Rather than toward the cave mouth, Anna had led Lamb deeper into the cave, surrounded by friendly and almost affectionate Draunskur.

They were brought to a cavern that rivaled the treasure chamber of Ali Baba's forty thieves. The room was filled with all manner of goods. There were weapons, armor, clothing, tents, blankets, rugs, and other equipment captured from travelers through the Endless Barrens.

"Take your pick," Anna said with a sweeping gesture. Harry glanced at her with amusement and noticed that she was now dressed and equipped almost exactly as she had been in Brian Teplow's drawings. He wondered if that had been deliberate, but what did it matter.

Lamb searched through a vast collection of weaponry. Among the swords, spears, and polearms of various sizes and shapes, he noted several of the mancatchers that the insect-men had carried. Buried in the armory, which was piled haphazardly on the floor of a cavern, Lamb was attracted to an ornate, golden baton that seemed out of place. One end was thinner than the other and ended in a blunted point. He picked up the baton, which was heavier than it looked. It must be some kind of club, he thought.

That is an energy weapon, the Draunskur voice said in his mind. *The minions of the sorcerer were granted their power. Only the faithful of Gho-Bazh have been known to make them work.*

Lamb kept the baton, but also picked up a small, recurved bow with a number of gears and levers to adjust and hold the tension. He took a quiver of arrows, and a short sword. He then rummaged through the hoard and found tough leather pants and a thick, but comfortable shirt. These he covered with armor similar to Anna's. Finally, he assembled a collection of blankets, water skins, and other assorted camping supplies.

As he gathered up the equipment, Lamb noticed Anna loading it into multiple sets of saddle bags, which the Draunskur then gathered up and walked off with.

"Where are they taking those?" Lamb asked with concern.

"It will be with our mounts when we arrive," Anna said with an expression Lamb could not decipher. "Trust me."

With the assistance of the small beings, Anna then led Lamb through a labyrinth of subterranean passages until they emerged into a pit surrounded by columns that was identical to the colonnaded Roman-style temple in the Church of Cosmic Understanding. Unlike the temple in New York, however, a stone staircase rose from the sandy pit to the gallery above.

They ascended the steps and Lamb realized that this was the where the cultists' ritual had brought them. Utgarda had arisen from the sandy floor of the pit. And Liv Lee had been flung from here into the Endless Barrens of None to become Queen Sif of Brynner.

Outside the temple, six of the flying Draunskur waited patiently. Lamb watched as Anna approached one. The creature hopped up and gently took hold of her shoulders. Its talons were long enough to completely encircle them. Then it and two of the others flew off.

Lamb was frozen in place. His feet would not respond when he commanded them to approach the creatures. One of the waiting flyers took wing and landed on his shoulders, wrapped its talons around them, and took off. Lamb flailed his arms as his feet left the ground. The two remaining flyers flanked him, and the three followed Anna and her escorts toward the setting sun.

◆

O'Malley shuddered as Lamb's viewpoint took flight and the landscape shrank below him. The image on the screen followed them above a vast, open wasteland toward high mountains. Anna dangled precariously in the talons of a winged creature reminiscent of the ones they had fought at the Church of Cosmic Understanding. Two others flew to either side as protection.

◆

As they traveled, Anna saw a large column of dark spots advancing across the empty landscape in the distance to her right. Each carried something that reflected the sunlight and they twinkled like stars. As she watched, dust kicked up around the column, and a large number of the flying Draunskur swooped in to attack.

An image appeared in her mind. It was the man in the red conical hat from Rose's cabinet at the Cavalier Club. He stood on a rise and watched the column of Pointees go by. He seemed to notice Anna, met her gaze and said, "Have you figured it out yet?"

◆

The flight must have been swift, because O'Malley got vertigo whenever Lamb looked down toward the blurry ground as it sped past far below. It seemed like an eternity, but the group started downward toward a pair of the six-legged mounts with the blade-like forelimbs. The beasts were fitted with saddles and multiple sets of saddlebags filled to overflowing with provisions.

Dozens of the small, large-eyed, large-eared beings wandered about the creatures, checking tack and other mundane tasks as the flyers approached and let go when their passengers' feet touched the ground.

◆

We can take you no farther, the Draunskur voice said in Lamb and Anna's heads. *The path you seek is just below*, and the two glanced toward a gentle slope before them. *It will take you to the sorcerer's realm. Fare well.*

Without hesitation, the flyers took to the air in the direction they had come from, while the assembly on the ground sank into the stone below their feet. In an instant, the two were alone with the shufflers.

"They certainly don't stand on ceremony," Lamb said, mounting one of the beasts. The six-limbed reptile-bird eyed him warily as he approached, but allowed him to climb onto its back.

"Indeed," Anna agreed, and mounted the other creature. "Our destiny awaits," she said as she willed the shuffler toward the slope. As she descended, Anna wondered why she had said that.

Lamb followed, and the beasts easily climbed down to a familiar-looking packed-earth path that now ran along the foot of the tall mountains on the other side. The gentle rise on their left was covered alternately with thick stands of trees and rocky outcroppings before the steep slopes of the mountains thrust up abruptly. On either side of the path, narrow but deep drainage channels paralleled it.

Without another word, Anna's mount reared up, its front two pairs of limbs thrust into the air, and then took off down the path. Lamb spurred his shuffler forward and followed at a gallop.

Chapter 15

?

Anna and Lamb rode single file with Anna in the lead. The shufflers had no reins. Instead, they seemed to know what was expected of them and responded to the squeezing and relaxing of their riders' legs. Lamb had heard somewhere that warhorses were trained to respond in this way so that riders could wield their weapons unimpeded.

The journey was pleasant, and the two were comfortable now that they were properly dressed. The path they followed was more evident now. The mountains that rose sharply on their left, and the slope up to the plateau on the right, sheltered the trail from the heat of the sun, and whatever moisture there was collected in the space in between. As a result, sparse lavender or pale purplish foliage grew on either side of the road, and here and there, trickles of water that flowed from the high slopes pooled in the gutters that ran parallel to the path.

"I suspect that we have climbed in elevation," Lamb said. "The temperature has dropped significantly."

"I would agree," Anna replied, turning back toward Lamb. "The air seems a little thinner here. It's harder to take a deep breath."

Lamb had not noticed the thinner atmosphere, but he had been raised in the mountains of upstate New York, while Anna had spent most of her life at sea level.

"Don't overexert yourself," he counseled. "It will take a few days to adjust. Let the shuffler do the work in the meantime."

"This is not a new experience for me," Anna replied. "I did fieldwork in the Caucasus Mountains for three years." She turned to face forward again. "You should take care yourself."

◆

"They seem to be back on track," O'Malley said in relief, taking a sip of tea. Anna and Lamb were now riding at a leisurely pace on a well-traveled road. Occasional travelers on wagons pulled by six-legged beasts passed in the other direction. The passersby avoided eye contact with the two, and only seemed to acknowledge the pair when Anna or Lamb addressed them.

"And they now resemble the figures in the drawings. Do you think that was deliberate or just coincidence?"

"I don't know," O'Malley replied conversationally. He had gotten accustomed to the situation, and sat comfortably in an old arm chair facing the display of Lamb's visual input. Billy had brought the chair from another part of the house. A tea set sat on a coffee table next to it. The center of the room now more resembled a comfortable living room than an alien laboratory.

"They have diverged from the story told in the sketchbook," O'Malley continued after taking a bite of a biscuit. "All of their companions in the drawings turned out to be adversaries. And there were no drawings of anyone else."

"It is a most curious turn of events," Bierce said from the table behind the priest. "The Junazhi tell me that they are learning a lot about shared subconscious experience."

"What do they do with this knowledge?"

"The Junazhi are a shared consciousness. What one knows, all know, as do those with whom they are linked, such as myself. I have learned things about the multiverse beyond human comprehension."

"Does Billy also have this knowledge?"

"Billy is not linked to the Junazhi consciousness. He is a servant. The Junazhi have dominated his mind and he performs as collective consciousness commands. He obeys me at their sufferance."

"I see," O'Malley said bitterly. "Billy is their slave."

"For lack of a better term, that is correct. He is not wholly controlled. He is free to do as he wishes unless given a task. The only thing he is required to do is protect the Junazhi from discovery."

◆

Two days had passed since their departure from the Draunskur. A train of wagons loaded with trade goods and pulled by female shufflers passed by heading toward Tiornen. Lamb noted that the wagons mostly carried metalworks. Pots, pans, iron stoves, and the like. Gho-Bazh's kingdom appeared to have a strong blacksmithing industry.

Anna attempted to greet the traders as they passed, but most ignored the two. The few that did respond only gestured politely, but with weapons visible. Anna imagined that the riders of the claw-limbed male shufflers were uncommon, though she thought she heard the name Nygof whispered on more than one occasion.

They continued on for several more hours. As they rounded a bend in the road, they saw a heavy wooden bridge which crossed a small stream. A few hundred feet off the path a waterfall cascaded down the sheer side of the mountain and collected in a clear pool the color of the sky. The water trickled down the slight slope, under the bridge, and disappeared into a hole on the other side of the road.

A young girl, perhaps ten or twelve years old, sat by the pool filling water skins. The leather bags were nearly as big as her, and a wooden yoke sat on a shoulder-high rack, clearly used to transport the filled water skins somewhere.

At the sound of their shuffler's footsteps, the girl looked toward the road and her face bloomed into a joyful smile.

"Nygof?" the girl cried, dropping the water skin in her hand into the pool and running toward the rider. Anna stopped her mount and looked back in surprise. The girl ran to her, unafraid of the shuffler's long claws, and leapt into Anna's lap in a single bound, hugging her tightly.

"It is you," she said, kissing Anna's lips and hugging her again. She spoke with the same accent as Anna. "I thought you had gone for good." Anna looked to Lamb, who shrugged. She returned the hug.

"We are on our way to Kreipsche," Anna said conversationally. "We have some business there." The girl looked up at Anna with a mischievous smile.

"I bet Father will not approve of this business," the girl said, "but we had better let him be the judge of that. Come on!" She hopped out of Anna's lap, running past the pond and up a trail into a stand of trees near the cliff face.

"I suppose we should look into this," Lamb said. "If you are known, we'd best find out what reputation you have around here."

"Those merchants were certainly not pleased to see me," Anna agreed. "Let us meet my family."

◆

"Papa! Papa! Nygof is home!" Anna followed the shouts of the girl through the copse to a clearing in which a log cabin and a barn stood. A handful of pig-like creatures wallowed nearby. They were pale blue in color, with large, darker-blue spots that somehow blended in against the mauve-colored mud.

Pale smoke billowed from the chimney of the cabin. The girl stood in the open doorway, looking back toward Anna.

"Sobak!" a husky male voice shouted from within. "Close the door. And where is the water?"

"Papa," the girl said over her shoulder, "look! Nygof is back!"

Anna stopped her mount, which she had named Mushta, and he laid down to allow her to dismount easily. She stroked his beak as a thick, burly, older man emerged from the cabin. The man was not familiar, but he rushed up to Anna, wrapped his arms around her, and squeezed her tightly.

Lamb was amused by Anna's discomfort. She did not enjoy such overt affection. But the doctor kept his expression to a pleased smile as he guided his mount over next to Anna's.

"Nygof," the man said with a grin, releasing his embrace and holding her by the shoulders to admire her. "You have become a beautiful woman." Then his expression became serious. "What brings you back to us?"

"Why must you interrogate her?" a stern, female voice said from the doorway. "She has only just arrived." The woman strode purposefully up and stood next to the man. She eyed Lamb suspiciously.

Sobak emerged from the barn carrying a pair of squirming, squealing bundles, which she deposited in front of each of the beasts. They were piglets whose legs had been bound together. As soon as she stepped away, she giggled as the shufflers snatched them up and swallowed them after only a couple of chews.

"And who is this? Have you finished with Dryagin already?" Sobak gave Anna a mischievous smile.

"But where are our manners?" the woman said, eying the girl reproachfully. She swept Anna from his grasp with a motherly arm around her waist and said, "Come and eat."

◆

"Those people are being awfully affectionate," O'Malley said, "but Anna does not seem to recognize them."

"Are they not her family?"

"Anna does not have any surviving family," O'Malley said. "And from what she has told me, she was not especially close to her parents. They sold her into marriage as a girl in exchange for passage to America."

"Then who are these people?"

"I think they are someone's conjecture of who her family might be."

"To what end?"

"And who dreamed them up?"

Chapter 16

?

"That armor makes you look half a head taller," the older woman said as she released Anna in the main room of the cabin. "Take off your traveling clothes so I can get a good look at you." Unconsciously, Anna slid out of her animal hide coat, and turned in place at the woman's gesture. As she did so, the cuffs on her wrists and ankles slid into view.

"Sobak, the water!" the man shouted over his shoulder before the girl entered the room. He closed the door and looked at Anna's shackles. "You were enslaved!" he said in astonishment. He grabbed her wrist to examine the cuff more closely.

"I was imprisoned by the Queen of Brynner," Anna said with a reassuring tone. "But the matter has been resolved and now I am free."

"If you are a free woman, why do you still wear the cuffs?" the man said with suspicious. He glanced at Lamb. "Is he your chaperone on some errand for this queen?"

"I facilitated her release," Lamb said with a friendly smile, holding out his hand. The older man eyed the hand suspiciously.

"So you have become his property," the man said with a scowl. He rounded on Lamb, but Anna grabbed the fist he intended to throw.

"I am not his slave," Anna said. "He talked the queen into giving us a task in exchange for our freedom. He is a good friend."

"I do not see cuffs on him," the man said, unswayed. "So who are you?"

"I am known as Nab here," Lamb said. "The queen confused me with someone else and used Ann, uh, Nygof here to pressure me into doing her bidding. I agreed in exchange for our freedom."

Just then, Sobak returned with the yoke over her shoulders and the heavy bags of water hanging from either side. She pushed the door open with the yoke and blindly sidestepped through the portal, knocking into Lamb, who fell into the older man's arms.

"Cover those up," the woman whispered to Anna, shielding her from the girl's view. "You do not want your sister to see them."

"Yes, Mother," Anna said reflexively, and bent over to stuff the ankle cuffs under the legs of her trousers. The wrist cuffs were too loose to hide under her shirt, so she pulled the sleeves over them and stuffed the ends underneath them. They looked odd, but at least they were out of sight.

Two more places were set at the central table, and the older man sat at the head. Sobak sat on one side, farthest from her father as if by rote, and gestured for Lamb to sit at the foot. Anna moved toward the opposite side of the table.

"You have forgotten your place already," the man said disappointedly, and leaned his head toward the seat next to the girl. Anna responded immediately and quickly sat in the indicated seat. Lamb followed suit.

"I hope there is enough," the woman said cheerfully, carrying an iron pot by a handle in a mittened hand. She ladled stew into the bowl before her husband, who continued to scowl as the woman moved on to Anna, then Sobak, and finally Lamb. When the doctor saw that the woman's bowl was only partially filled, he offered his portion to her, but she declined.

"So where have you been?" Sobak asked Anna with youthful enthusiasm. "Where are you off to now?" Then she whispered, "Is he your new man?"

"One question at a time, Sobak," the woman mock-scolded. "Give your sister time to collect her thoughts." She looked at Anna with a "tell a story suitable for her" expression.

"Well, uh," Anna started, "we just came from Brynner, where, um, we were trading, um, pots and pans-"

"You do not have to clean it up for me," the girl said in irritation, "I have had twelve winters. I will probably be married off before I see you again."

"We can only hope," her father said brusquely. "We must live here, in the shadow of demons, because of your reputation," he said to Anna. "Nygof the assassin. Nygof the thief. Nygof the spy. Sobak will be lucky to be taken by a sheep herder." He stabbed hard at a chunk of meat in his bowl and thrust it into his mouth. "Why do you come to us now?"

"We were just passing by," Anna said anxiously. She did not know why she was deferring to this man. He was not her father. She had never seen any of these people before. Why did it seem so natural and appropriate? "We are en route to Kreipsche," she replied with annoyance as she stood. "We did not intend to impose on you," she looked about for her coat, "so we will leave you in peace!" The man huffed, but the woman grabbed Lamb's wrist as he started to rise.

"You must stay the night," she said pleadingly. "It will be cold and dark, and I bet you have not slept comfortably since you left the city." She turned to the man with an expression demanding agreement. He nodded reluctantly.

"Yes," he said, "of course. You must rest your mounts." He looked at Lamb. "You will stay in the barn," he said to the doctor, "and you, Nygof, will take your bed with your sister." Sobak beamed with joy and took Anna's hand.

"Come on," the girl said as she started to pull Anna away.

"After we eat," the woman said with a satisfied smile. "Sit and finish your food."

◆

Nygof's father sat with Lamb on a log in front of the barn. They had led the shufflers into stalls, and once they were settled came outside, where the old man lit a long-stemmed pipe.

The older man still did not like him, but he behaved civilly at his wife's insistence. The meal was completed in an awkward silence before Sobak took Nygof up a ladder, presumably to their sleeping chamber.

"You will take good care of my daughter," the old man said with parental concern. "She is wild and independent, and requires a strong hand. But do not mistreat her, or-" He trailed off introspectively.

"Nygof and I are just business associates," Lamb said reassuringly. "There is nothing between us otherwise." He stared earnestly into the old man's eyes. The latter stared back for a few moments, and then nodded with resignation.

"This way," he said, rising and gesturing toward the barn. Lamb rose as well and followed him back inside. He showed

Lamb the ladder to the loft. "Unlike what you might expect, it gets quite warm up there, so you should be comfortable." He paused, and then patted Lamb's shoulder gently, turned, and left the barn.

Lamb climbed the ladder and discovered a thick cushion of fresh hay. He would have been confident that he would be eaten alive by insects, except that he had not seen any insects since he appeared in Sif's palace.

Lamb smiled. The old man thought he and Anna were lovers. At least he had convinced the old man that his daughter was not Nab's slave. He wondered if wives were considered property there. Musing on that thought, he laid down in the rather comfortable hay. It was indeed warm. Perhaps caused by decomposition-

◆

"Come on," Sobak said as she climbed onto the bed and nestled against the wall. "I am bigger now, so there will not be as much room, but we can cuddle like we used to, before-" Her voice choked off with a whimper and she turned to face the wall.

"Before what?" Anna said, sitting on the bed beside her. Instinctively, she stroked the girl's long blond hair. Sobak turned back toward Anna and put her arms around the older woman.

"Before you ran off and became a slave," Sobak said meekly, pulling the cuff out from Anna's sleeve. "Did you escape? Are slave hunters going to come after you? Is that why you have to leave me again?" She buried her face in Anna's lap.

"It is like I told you at dinner," Anna said softly. "Nab and I are doing an errand for the Queen of Brynner. That's all."

"Then why do you still have those?" Sobak asked, examining one of the irons. "There is no lock. How do they come off?" Anna gave her a knowing look. "Oh," the girl said, "they do not come off!" She looked closer at the iron. "Is it too thick to cut?"

"It would probably just be easier to cut off my hand," Anna said with a sisterly grin. "But that is a topic for another time. We must sleep now."

Sobak pressed herself against the wall to make the most space on the bed and patted it cloth-covered straw. Anna laid down, and the girl threw her arm around Anna's waist and pressed her head into Anna's hair.

◆

The man in the conical hat leered at Anna and laughed maniacally. He stood next to the bed flanked by two Pointees.

Anna woke with a start. There was a commotion in the room below. She rose quietly, lifted the trapdoor in the floor a crack, and peered through. Half a dozen Pointees were searching the rooms below. There was no sign of her parents.

Anna quietly closed the hatch and tiptoed back to the bed.

"Sobak, wake up," she said as she gently shook the girl's shoulder. Sobak rolled over lazily and faced the wall.

"Sobak!" Anna said quietly, but with more urgency. "We have to get out of here!"

"What is it?" Sobak said wearily as she silently yawned and stretched.

"There are intruders searching the house," Anna whispered. The crash of breaking dishes roused the girl from her stupor.

Anna scanned the small room. The only other exit was a small window. She padded over to it and saw the barn a short distance away. A moment later, the door of the loft opened inward a crack and Anna saw Lamb peer out.

They made eye contact. Anna scanned the ground below, but there were no signs of other intruders. When she looked to Lamb again, he has his bow in hand. He showed Anna an arrow with a thin rope attached. He wanted her to use the rope to cross the gap.

Anna shook her head, but the arrow struck the cabin solidly and the rope went taut. Sobak appeared by her side and hugged her waist.

"We need to use the rope to get to the barn," Anna said with confidence. "Do you think you can do it?" Sobak eyed the rope and saw Lamb gesturing to come to him. Then she looked down and gulped.

"I do not know how," the girl said. Anna weighed her options.

"Do you want me to go first?" she said with concern. When Sobak nodded, she said, "All right. But you must follow as soon as I reach the barn!"

Sobak nodded with reservation, but there was no more time for debate. The Pointees would check the attic at any moment.

Anna tested the line, and it was taut. The rope was looped through a hole in the arrowhead for that purpose, and both were firmly embedded in the wall.

"Watch how I do it," Anna said. She grabbed hold of the rope, pulled herself out a little, and then wrapped one leg and then the other around it, hanging upside down. "Do exactly as I do once I reach the other side."

◆

O'Malley was amazed at Anna's agility as she seemed to effortlessly cross the gap to the barn. In less than a minute, she had crossed what appeared to be a ten-foot gap and slid into the barn.

Lamb looked back at the window where the young girl stood with wide eyes. He gestured for her to come to him.

Anna stepped in front of him and took up the encouragement.

Slowly, the girl reached up and took hold of the rope. She looked down and froze, then looked back into the room. With renewed vigor, the girl jumped up, but missed the top with her leg. She looked into the room again, and then leapt up and wrapped both legs around the rope at once.

◆

"You are doing fine, Sobak," Anna said quietly.

"They are coming," the girl replied. "I put the bar across the door, but they were trying to break through!"

"Concentrate!" Anna said. "You are already halfway across!"

Suddenly there was a crash from the attic room and Sobak was distracted. She lost her grip and fell with a scream.

Chapter 17

?

Anna watched Sobak fall. The girl's arms flailed, and her wide eyes locked on Anna's. Anna turned away before she hit the ground.

"KHAN-TRAL HAS GOT YOU!" a loud, strong voice shouted from below. Anna opened her eyes to see a tall, muscular man dressed only in a fur-covered loincloth holding Sobak in both arms. He sat upon a female shuffler, and a long, wide sword lay in a scabbard across his back.

Lamb yanked on the arrow, but it did not budge, and a horned warrior bellowed as it peered out of the window after the girl.

"Come on," Lamb said, grabbing Anna's arm as he headed toward the ladder. She looked back, noticing how handsome the bare-chested rider was, then shook her head vigorously to clear the thought and followed the doctor down the ladder.

As she reached the bottom, Anna was amazed as Lamb drew and fired off three arrows in rapid succession. She followed their path and saw an arrow strike each of the horned warriors in the head. The muscle-bound warrior had dismounted, leaving the stunned Sobak on his mount's back, and was cleaving through the warriors that Lamb had shot, his two-handed sword slicing one of them in half.

"KHAN-TRAL DEALT THE FINAL BLOW, SO THE KILLS ARE HIS!" the swordsman shouted as he turned and winked at Anna.

Sobak met Anna's gaze with a wide smile and mouthed "Wow!" and turned to admire the handsome warrior who had saved her.

"KHAN-TRAL WILL HANDLE THIS," he said as he stormed into the cabin. There was a commotion, and the old woman climbed awkwardly out of a window, pushed from behind by her husband, who disappeared out of view back inside and then flew out the window himself. Then there was silence.

The warrior emerged from the cabin carrying a dead Pointee in each hand and one over his shoulder. He dumped them on top of the other three. Then he lifted Sobak off the shuffler. She wrapped her arms around his neck, her legs around his chest, and kissed him on the lips. The warrior politely pulled her away, set her down on her feet, and nudged toward her mother, who ran to meet her with tears in her eyes.

Her father surveyed the carnage all around in shock, and stumbled toward the warrior. Anna and Lamb emerged from the barn and rushed to join them.

"We are in your debt–" the old man started to say sheepishly to the giant before him.

"NONSENSE," the warrior shouted, and Anna realized that that was his normal speaking voice. "THERE IS NO NEED FOR GRATITUDE. KHAN-TRAL'S PURPOSE IS TO SLAY THESE FOUL BEAST-MEN!"

"You are Khan-Tral," Anna said, "the companion of Deb-Roh?"

"KHAN-TRAL AND DEB-ROH ARE BLOOD BROTHERS," the warrior shouted, smiling as he looked over Anna. "BUT THEY HAVE NOT TRAVELED TOGETHER SINCE DEB RAN AFOUL OF THE WIZARD."

"You mean Gho-Bazh," Lamb said. A brief look of annoyance shot across Khan-Tral's face as he turned from Anna to Lamb, but his infectious geniality and confidence returned immediately.

"KHAN-TRAL IS NOT A FRIEND OF THE WIZARD WHO HAS ENCHANTED HIS FRIEND AND FELLOW TRAVELER. HIS JOURNEYS HAVE BEEN LONELY AND DULL THESE PAST FEW MONTHS." He smiled back at Anna again. "UNTIL TODAY. PERHAPS THIS BEAUTIFUL BLOOM BRINGS A CHANGE OF FORTUNE WITH HER."

Sobak, forgotten by the others, huffed with disappointment at the handsome warrior's clear interest in her older sister. Khan-Tral looked down, smiled to the girl, and tousled her hair. She was not amused.

"Nevertheless," her father continued, "we thank the gods for sending you to us." He looked disappointingly toward Anna and Lamb, "Thank you for killing these cursed beast-men before they destroyed our home." Anna opened her mouth to speak, but Khan-Tral spoke first.

"KHAN-TRAL COULD NOT HAVE DEALT WITH THE FOE WERE IT NOT FOR THE QUICK THINKING OF YOUR DAUGHTER AND THE MARKSMAN FROM THE BARN." He took Lamb's arm in a gesture of camaraderie. "HAD THEY NOT SEEN TO THE GIRL, KHAN-TRAL WOULD HAVE HAD TO DELAY HIS ASSAULT UNTIL THEY WERE SAFE."

"Still," the woman said, standing behind Sobak with her hands on the girl's shoulders, "we owe you our gratitude. You must accept a meal from us." The warrior glanced from the woman, to the man, to Anna, to Sobek, and finally to Lamb, and then shrugged.

"IF IT PLEASES YOU," he said genially, "KHAN-TRAL WILL DINE, SO LONG AS THIS PRETTY YOUNG ONE SITS WITH ME." Sobak blushed and giggled, then broke free of her mother's grip, took the warrior's hand, and tried to lead him toward the door. "BUT FIRST WE MUST DEAL WITH THIS MESS."

◆

Khan-Tral insisted on carrying the bodies of the dead beast-men across the road and up onto the Endless Barrens of None. There, he stood in silence with his arms crossed as the corpses burned brightly just before the sun rose. Anna and Lamb stood at the lip of the rise and watched him.

For the first time, the enormous warrior was silent. Lamb kept his bow at the ready and scanned the wasteland before them for any signs of trouble. Anna found herself admiring Khan-Tral's broad shoulders and bulging muscles. His shoulder-length black hair blew agreeably in the warm breeze. She sighed with a smile.

Khan-Tral turned toward her at the sound and smiled lustily. He motioned for her to join him by the pyre. Anna blushed and giggled quietly. Then she padded over to the warrior.

"Khan-Tral is pleased that you accepted his offer," the warrior said loudly, but not shouting, with a knowing smile.

"So you do have a lower volume," Anna replied, meeting his gaze with a smile of her own.

"How do you find yourself under his control?" Khan-Tral gestured toward Lamb, who remained concealed at the lip of the plain, and then at her wrist cuffs. "It does not suit you."

"I am not his property," Anna replied quietly, but with irritation. "We are traveling together to do a job!" She crossed her arms. "Why does everyone think I am his slave? Do I appear to be servile?"

"There are slaves," he said, peering down into her eyes, "who serve as more than just companions. They are given great latitude. Some even have slaves of their own."

"I am not a slave," Anna said, clearly annoyed now. She heard Lamb approaching quickly. "Nab and I have been sent on an errand in exchange for our freedom."

"An errand for who?" Khan-Tral asked curiously.

"We have been tasked by Queen Sif of Brynner with killing the sorcerer, Gho-Bazh," Lamb said abruptly. Anna detected jealousy in his voice and noticed that the doctor was standing very close to her. She found herself pleasantly amused.

"You would seek to kill the wizard?" Khan-Tral chuckled. Then he thought for a moment. "And you would go to his palace to do so?" He doubled over with laughter.

"Yes," Lamb replied in a tone of superiority. Anna looked at him in curiosity.

"We are actually seeking to rescue Deb-Roh," Anna said. "Queen Sif's mission was merely a means to an end."

Khan-Tral sobered and scrutinized Anna, and then Lamb. He kept his gaze on the two for a long moment, and then grinned.

"You would release Khan-Tral's blood brother from the wizard?" he said with a smile. Then his expression turned sour. "And how would you seek to dispel the enchantments that hold Deb-Roh prisoner?"

"We have not worked that out yet," Anna said.

"Our understanding is that killing the wizard will break his spells," Lamb replied pointedly. "Once Gho-Bazh has fallen by my bow, Deb-Roh will be free." Anna found herself attracted to Lamb's confidence and posturing.

"Then Khan-Tral will lend Nightbane, the Razor of Delusions, to the task." He drew his sword, knelt before Anna, held it out before him in both hands, and smiled at her.

Then he stood abruptly, sheathed the sword, gave Lamb a look of superiority, and returned toward the escarpment and the cabin.

◆

The meal was awkward. Anna sat next to Lamb and found herself glancing at Khan-Tral, much to annoyance of Sobak, who was sitting next to him. At the same time, Lamb continually closed the gap between him and Anna until they were touching. The tension in the room was amplified by the lack of any conversation.

Anna slid away from Lamb and broke the silence. "What brought you here?"

"KHAN-TRAL GOES WHERE THE ROAD TAKES HIM." As soon as they had left the Endless Barrens of None, he had resumed shouting.

"No," Anna said. "I mean what brought you down this road, to this farm, at this time?"

"FATE," the warrior replied simply, but then added, "AND I SAW A BAND OF BEAST-MEN COMING DOWN THE ROAD. THEY STARTED SNEAKING ABOUT WHEN THEY GOT CLOSE TO THIS HOUSE."

"So the Pointees were coming here," Lamb said suspiciously. "Could they have known where we were?"

"So now you have angered the Red Wizard!" the old man said. "What more is there to your tale?"

"THEY INTEND TO KILL HIM AND RESCUE DEB-ROH," Khan-Tral shouted conversationally. "A WORTHY QUEST! NIGHTBANE, THE RAZOR OF DELUSIONS, WILL FEAST ON THEIR FOES."

"You have brought the wrath of the Red Wizard on our house," Nygof's father growled. "First we have to abandon our lives because of you to live alone in this wasteland, and now the Red Wizard, of all people has sent his soldiers to attack us. So we must again find a new safe haven elsewhere." He glared at Anna. "Where are we to go, Nygof? The Endless Barrens? We can't go to a city! We will be found there for sure."

"FEAR NOT," the warrior shouted as he stood and drew his sword. "KHAN-TRAL AND HIS COMPANIONS WILL KILL GHO-BAZH AND END THE RED WIZARD'S TYRANNY!"

"We are not your companions," Lamb said pointedly as he stood. "It is our mission and we are letting you accompany us."

"ONLY BECAUSE YOU NEED KHAN-TRAL'S SWORD, ARCHER!" Lamb noted his glance toward Anna. "WE WILL SEE WHO CLAIMS THE PRIZE!"

"Enough!" Anna said, standing herself. "We must work together if this mission is to succeed. It matters not who kills Gho-Bazh so long as Deb-Roh is released from his prison." She turned toward the old woman. "Thank you for sheltering and feeding us. We will take our leave now."

Before anyone else could speak, Anna walked outside and slammed the door, which flew open again after slamming Sobak in the face. Her nose bled as she ran to Anna and embraced her.

"You can't leave me again, Nygof," the girl cried. "You only just got here. And if we have to leave, you won't know where to find us." She sobbed, leaving wet spots where her eyes and mouth pressed into Anna's shirt. Anna hugged Sobak back.

"I have to go," she said compassionately. "We have a job to do," she paused, noted Lamb carrying her coat through the door, "and we are not welcome here." She held the girl at arm's length and looked into her eyes. "I will find you, wherever you are," she lied. She never expected to see the girl again, but she needed to escape that house.

"Do you promise?" Sobak said through her tears.

"We will meet again," Anna said with a hopeful expression. Sobak wiped the tears from her eyes, but then embraced Anna again.

"I love you, Nygof." Anna choked up. She did not have any real siblings, but this felt so real. She kissed the top of Sobak's head and separated from her. Anna walked toward the barn, following the men, but turned back to see Sobak, now flanked by her stoic parents, watching mutely.

Chapter 18

?

They traveled up the road in silence for several hours. Both of the men pressed increasingly closer to Anna as time passed. On two occasions, Khal-Tral and Lamb argued over who detected an oncoming wagon, and at Anna's insistence, the trio hid in the neighboring foliage until they had gone by.

The continued posturing made both of them less attractive to Anna, who began to wonder where her lust had come from in the first place. She had never been attracted to the doctor, and the muscle-bound warrior was so conceited that she could feel it if she concentrated on ignoring his physique. Finally she had had enough.

"I do not know what is happening here-" she started to say.

"Khan-Tral thinks it is quite clear," Khan-Tral said seductively.

"I doubt that," Lamb retorted as he moved his shuffler closer to the swordsman.

"Enough already," she spat, putting herself and her mount between them. "I do not know what is happening here," she repeated angrily, "but the flirtation and competition must stop now!"

She looked from Khan-Tral to Lamb. The warrior bore an expression of amused disbelief. The doctor was still focused on the swordsman.

"I am not interested in either of you. We have to work together on this mission. That is all." She turned suddenly to Khan-Tral, raising her finger, "And there will be nothing more after it is completed!"

For the first time since they had met him, the swordsman was speechless. Lamb was also silent and bore a hurt expression.

Anna softened and put her hand on Lamb's cheek. "Harry, we are the closest of friends and colleagues, but that is all. We must get Brian home to his mother."

She turned to Khan-Tral. "We need your help to rescue Deb-Roh. But I am not a prize to be won." She put up her finger to silence his interruption. "We do not belong here," she said, indicating Lamb and herself. "We need to find Brian Teplow and bring him home with us. But we don't even know where to begin."

"Who commands you to kill the Red Wizard?"

"Queen Sif of Brynner had me imprisoned," Anna said, displaying the irons on her wrists. "Nab secured my release in exchange for killing Gho-Bazh. We escaped our minders."

"SIF IS THE CAUSE OF YOUR TORMENT?" Anna nodded. "THAT WOMAN IS THE ROOT OF THE RIFT BETWEEN MY BROTHER AND I."

"You know Sif?" Lamb asked, his jealousy renewed.

"KHAN-TRAL AND DEB-ROH FOUND HER CRAWLING THROUGH THE ENDLESS BARRENS OF NONE. THEY HELPED SAVED HER FROM THE BEAST-MEN, BUT SIF ENSORCELLED DEB-ROH

AND DROVE THEM APART. WHEN KHAN-TRAL'S BROTHER WAS IN GHO-BAZH'S CLUTCHES, THE RED WIZARD CAST SIF ASIDE, AND NOW SHE IS AN ABOMINATION."

"You met her when she first arrived here," Lamb said softly.

"She was a beautiful woman when they found her. She changed into that creature after Gho-Bazh got his prize."

"So she was a lure to capture Deb-Roh," Anna said speculatively. "Perhaps you know other details that could be useful to us. What can you tell us about Kreipsche and Gho-Bazh's palace?"

◆

"I knew he looked familiar," O'Malley cried after concentrating on the muscle-bound swordsman. "I killed that man at the agent's apartment."

"It would appear that his counterpart survives here," the voice from the cylinder said.

"He summoned a monster to attack me, but I shot him before it arrived. His name was Gulden."

"He seems to be assisting your friends now."

"Indeed." O'Malley was curious about the juxtaposition of the players as compared to the accounts of Brian Teplow. "If I understand correctly, Anna and Harry have been transported to Brian Teplow's subconscious."

"That is not correct. They are in an actual realm of his creation."

"But he is the author of all," the priest asserted.

"As you have said previously, people and events have been altered from Teplow's account. You said that his allies have become adversaries. Perhaps the opposition is now on their side."

"Or they are on the wrong side-" O'Malley mused. Perhaps the goals of the Junazhi were contrary to Brian's. What if Anna and Lamb were inadvertently making things worse?

"The Junazhi are impartial," Bierce said. O'Malley had forgotten that the mind in the can could read his surface thoughts. "They know nothing of young Teplow's intentions or desires."

"Are you certain of that?" O'Malley queried. "How do you know *you* are completely clued in?"

"You raise a valid conjecture, Father O'Malley. It is possible that the Junazhi have concealed information from me. However, my interpretation of how their collective mind works is that concealing thought is beyond them. Still, it is possible that there are things pertaining to this endeavor that I myself do not understand. I will pursue this inquiry."

With that, the lights of the sensory device attached to the cylinder started flashing rapidly. The pulses were so bright and quick that O'Malley had to look away before they made his head hurt. Instead, he turned back to the image Lamb was providing.

◆

Over the next few days, Khan-Tral told the others what he knew of the Red Wizard and his kingdom. Kreipsche was not a city as much as it was an enormous fortress. It ran parallel to the River of Misgiving, which flowed into the Sea of Plenty. The walls of the fortress were thirty arm-spans tall and twenty arm-spans thick.

The palace was a massive keep in the center of the fortress complex. It was also surrounded by an equally high wall, with an open courtyard on all sides. The square tower was five stories tall. Untold magics defended the keep itself, but the fortress was guarded by a legion of beast-men armed with the energy sticks.

"Do you have any knowledge as to where Deb-Roh might be kept?" Lamb asked. Since Anna's declaration, the two had become more constructive than adversarial.

"And do you know of any ways into the fortress where we might not be seen," Anna added.

"THE RED WIZARD SEES DEB-ROH AS A GREAT PRIZE," Khan-Tral said. "KHAN-TRAL HAS HEARD RUMORS THAT HIS BROTHER IS ON DISPLAY IN THE THRONE ROOM."

"On display?" Lamb asked.

"SO HE HAS HEARD. KHAN-TRAL DOES NOT KNOW WHAT THAT MEANS."

"That means that we will need to go to the throne room and find out," Anna said flatly. "A dungeon might have been easier."

"Indeed," the swordsman mused quietly. "If he were in the dungeon, we could use the catacombs to get inside."

"There are catacombs?" Anna asked.

"Why yes. But they don't go into the keep, only to the dungeons."

"But they would get us within the walls," Lamb said, matching Anna's enthusiasm.

"True," Khan-Tral considered. "Of course, they go into a cell. We would then need to escape from that. The tunnels were designed for getting out, not getting in." He thought for a moment. "That's assuming that they have not been blocked, and that we can get past the traps and monsters that lurk there."

"How much longer would these catacombs take than continuing on the road?" Anna asked.

"IT MIGHT BE QUICKER," Khan-Tral said. "IF WE TAKE THE ROAD, WE HAVE TO GO ALL THE WAY AROUND THE NORTHERN END OF THE

GROANING SLOPES OF WOE." He indicated the mountains that rose steeply on their left just beyond the narrow band of trees. "THE CATACOMBS RUN THROUGH THE MOUNTAINS THEMSELVES." He considered the route. "YES, KHAN-TRAL THINKS THE CATACOMBS COULD BE MUCH FASTER."

"What kinds of traps and monsters?" Lamb asked cautiously.

"NOTHING WE THREE CAN'T HANDLE!" the warrior replied, exuding confidence.

"And these catacombs go through the mountains?" Anna asked. She had been on several archaeological expeditions in mountainous terrain, and mountain ranges tended to actually be wider than they were high in most cases. The few exceptions she knew of were where some of the peaks had collapsed into a neighboring sea.

"Indeed."

"Where do we find the entrance to these catacombs?" Lamb asked.

"Khan-Tral knows the way," Khan-Tral said with confidence. "That's how he rescued Deb-Roh last time."

"You have rescued Deb-Roh from Gho-Bazh before?" Anna asked with suspicion.

"Of course," the warrior replied. "Khan-Tral and Deb-Roh sought renown by challenging the Red Wizard in his lair. They failed, then escaped from the dungeon through the catacombs. That was before Gho-Bazh knew who Deb-Roh was."

"And he sent Sif to lure you back," Anna deduced to the swordsman's surprise.

"Just so," Khan-Tral replied in amazement. "How did you know?"

"I read this story in one of Brian's journals," she said. "But in that tale, you and Deb-Roh separated because you were jealous of Sif's affection for him."

"That is a fiction. Khan-Tral and Deb-Roh are as one. That temptress lured him with her wiles and gave him to the wizard."

"And only he was taken with her?" Lamb asked. Khan-Tral hesitated uncharacteristically. "If we are to put our lives in your hands, we must trust each other."

"Very well," the warrior conceded. "We were both captivated by her, but Khan-Tral was the stronger of them, and he managed to break free of the spell. Deb-Roh was thoroughly under her power. In the end, Khan-Tral had to bind and gag Deb-Roh and carry him through the catacombs until the spell wore off."

"Or you were far enough away," Anna said, remembering Lamb in Sif's palace. "Her magics must have a limited range."

"If we are to take to the catacombs, we will need some supplies," Khan-Tral said. "We will need light, a lot of rope, and rations." He paused with a frown. "And we will have to leave our mounts behind." He patted his shuffler's flank with unexpected affection.

"And how are we to acquire these supplies?" Anna asked. "We have no money with which to pay for anything."

"And we don't want to be seen," Lamb added.

"We will have to *borrow* what we need from those who have it," Khan-Tral replied coolly.

"You mean steal it," Anna spat.

"It happens all the time," Khan-Tral replied. "Invading armies take whatever they want. We will take only what we need."

"How do we know we will even find anyone else on this road?" Lamb asked.

"This is the only road from Kreipsche to Tiornen. All traders who do not go by sea must travel this way. There are a few trading posts along our path before we head for the entrance to the catacombs."

"We really have no other choice," Anna conceded.

"On the other hand," Lamb mused, "if we *are* sighted in this area, Gho-Bazh might send more of his forces to look for us here." He turned to Khan-Tral. "How many know of these catacombs?"

"Few are aware of them, and even fewer have passed through."

"Then this sounds like a good plan," Anna said. "We will make our presence known in this area, and then we will disappear, only to reappear in the fortress itself."

Chapter 19

?

"KNOW THAT THE ASSISTANCE YOU GIVE KHAN-TRAL AND HIS COMPANIONS WILL AID IN ENDING THE TYRANNY OF THE RED WIZARD!"

The phrase was getting bothersome to Anna and Lamb since the swordsman shouted it every time they left one of the homesteads of trading posts they raided. They tried to leave game or trade goods they didn't actually need that had been taken from other raids to conceal their plans, but as their required supplies increased, there was less space to carry extraneous things.

They spent several days traveling up and back down the road, stopping at alternating settlements each time. At the last trading post, the farthest point north that they had intended to go, the inhabitants had been prepared as word had spread of the marauding band in the area.

As expected, the simple folk were neither skilled fighters or well-equipped. The three put up a show of being repelled by the defenders and pursued into the wilderness, but evaded the angry folk easily enough. Word would surely spread to Gho-Bazh that they were in the area and out for his head.

They had acquired torches, a large quantity of oil, several hundred feet of rope, spikes used for mountain climbing, and a goodly supply of dried meat. Lamb had also acquired, at Khan-Tral's suggestion, a large quantity of metal arrowheads, which the warrior pounded holes through so that they could be used to shoot ropes into distant stone.

"Your bow will not be very useful for combat down below," the swordsman had said, "but it will be essential if we are to cross chasms or climb sheer chimneys. The only things plentiful in the catacombs are water and danger. Whatever else we need, we will have to bring in on our backs."

The muscled giant was not daunted by the sheer weight and bulk of what they had assembled, but Anna and Lamb doubted that they would be able to carry it all.

"The most important things are the lanterns and the oil," the warrior replied. "There is water, and we can do without food for a while, or eat the denizens of the dark if we must, but without light we will be helpless." He eyed the two. "Unless either of you can naturally see in total darkness."

"I am afraid that neither of us are so gifted," Anna replied.

"I think this will be a new experience for both of us," Lamb added.

"I have been in underground tombs and catacombs before," Anna said, "so I have some idea of what to expect."

"You may be surprised," Khan-Trail said.

"When will we reach the entrance to the catacombs?" Anna asked.

"We will access them through an abandoned mine not far from here," Khan-Tral said.

"How do you know it is still abandoned?" Lamb asked.

"When the miners broke through to the tunnels below," the warrior said, "the denizens of that dark realm emerged and decimated them. The mine was abandoned and sealed."

"Then how are we to get in?" Anna asked.

"Khan-Tral and Deb-Roh came upon the fallen rock of a collapsed tunnel in their escape from the Red Wizard. With no other recourse, they dug their way through it, and eventually found the surface world once again. They plugged the entrance behind them to prevent the escape of the abominations from below, but Khan-Tral can open it."

"All right, then," Lamb said, "how far is this mine from here?"

"It is but a two day ride through the broken country," the swordsman said. "We will stay off the road so that we are not seen."

◆

"Where are they going?" O'Malley asked, watching as the three made their way along the side of a sheer cliff.

"They appear to be looking for something."

'True. The big one keeps searching in caves and cracks."

◆

Khan-Tral walked next to his mount and looked into every opening in the side of the mountains, going so far as to move stones here and there. Anna and Lamb kept watch for any onlookers as he probed, but the swordsman made no attempts at stealth.

"Should we not be more clandestine?" Anna asked the warrior after he threw a large rock into the trees, scattering a flock of birds. "If anyone is nearby, they have surely been alerted to our presence by now."

"There is no one within a day of this location," Khan-Tral said confidently. "We are far from the road and the land here is too rocky and broken for farming."

"What of hunters or herders?" Lamb asked. "I have noted footprints here and there." This caused the warrior some consternation.

"That is a valid concern," Anna agreed. "Wanderers or refugees might find such a remote place ideal." The swordsman stopped mid-throw and set the stone in his hand on the ground out of the way.

"Khan-Tral must confess that the landscape has changed somewhat since he was last here."

"And when was that?" Lamb asked.

"Khan-Tral and Deb-Roh escaped the Red Wizard just before the first thaws."

"So the ground was covered with snow and leafless trees," Lamb said in irritation. The warrior shrugged.

They continued on in to a copse of trees and around an outcropping when Khan-Tral stopped abruptly and signaled for silence. Quietly, Anna and Lamb dismounted and joined him at the end of the foliage.

About twenty feet away was another outcropping. Between the two arms of the cliff were the remnants of a rockslide that nearly filled the space, but Khan-Tral pointed to a small opening where the rockslide met the wall they now stood by. It was carefully concealed such that it would only be visible from their perspective, and it was large enough for even the giant warrior to squeeze through.

"That is the entrance to the mine," Khan-Tral whispered, "but it seems that it has been reopened recently. Perhaps the abominations have escaped."

"From the foot traffic," Lamb said, studying the ground, "I would say that there are people in there, and they probably come out to hunt fairly regularly." He gestured to the ground, but the others could not see the tracks until he pointed them out.

"In any case," Khan-Tral said, "our point of entry has been discovered. We must assume that those within are hostile, and possibly in the employ of the Red Wizard. Be ready."

"I suggest that we reconnoiter first before unloading the supplies," Lamb said, readying his bow.

"KHAN-TRAL WILL SURV-" the warrior shouted before Anna and Lamb pulled him back deeper into the copse.

"Perhaps stealth would be a better approach at this time," Anna scolded, putting her finger before her mouth for silence. "Cover me," she said, drawing a pair of knives from her bandoleer before sneaking forward out of the copse toward the opening.

Anna caught herself unconsciously twirling the blades around her fingers as she tiptoed toward the gap. Since they had left Sobak and "her" parents at the cabin, she had considered who they might be, or more precisely, how they came to be. Anna and Lamb were, after all, traveling in a realm of Brian Teplow's imagination.

She concluded that Brian's version of things was being influenced. They knew that Kovacs had hijacked the spiritualist's dream world, but a family for Nygof was too mundane for the sorcerer to have inserted. Anna considered that perhaps the figures had come from her own imagination, but she had never had any familial inclinations of any kind, so that could not have been it.

Anna focused again as she rounded a boulder that concealed the opening of the cave from someone facing the cliff. The opening was about three feet in diameter. There was weathered rubble on the ground which suggested that stones had been broken, perhaps by hammers.

Maybe some miners had returned. But if that were the case, the mine was not being worked. The entrance was deliberately concealed. It was more likely someone's hiding place. She grabbed the knives tightly in each hand and padded toward the opening. There were no sounds coming from within, and she did not smell anything unusual.

Anna glanced back toward the trees and saw Lamb with an arrow nocked in his bow. Carefully, she stepped forward. The little light that penetrated the hole revealed little. Just as she reached the threshold, a slab of polished stone in the floor reflected sunlight into her face, blinding her. Anna fell backward, shielding her eyes with her arms.

At the sight of Anna, Lamb took aim toward the gap, but Khan-Tral leaped forward into his line of sight. Lamb followed a moment later and joined the swordsman at Anna's side.

"What happened?" Lamb asked, moving Anna's arms to examine her eyes.

"There is a mirrored stone set in the floor at the entrance," Anna said as Lamb opened each eye to look closer. "It seems to be angled to catch sunlight and blind whoever approaches."

"A cunning trap," the warrior said. He pointed up to where another shiny slab was set into the wall and angled toward the one at the entrance. "Anyone who approaches must go down this narrow passage. Undoubtedly more treachery awaits beyond the threshold."

"Your eyes look fine," Lamb said in a professional tone.

"Khan-Tral agrees," the warrior said with a smile.

"I mean there doesn't appear to be any damage-"

"I know what you meant, doctor," Anna said. "The trap is designed to impair seeing in the dark. I have seen similar devices in tombs. I expect that the terrain within is dangerous enough that impairing vision would be sufficient to eliminate trespassers." Anna waited under Lamb's observation until her vision cleared.

While they sat, Khan-Tral eyed the reflective stone in the cliff face. He scooped up a large handful of dirt and sand from the ground and tossed it to where he estimated its counterpart would be. He then stepped forward with his hand out, looking for light reflected onto it. When he saw none, he peered within the cave.

"THERE IS INDEED A GREAT CHASM IMMEDIATELY TO THE RIGHT OF THE ENTRANCE," the warriors voice echoed from within. "TREAD CAREFULLY."

"We better get in there," Anna said. Lamb offered his assistance, but she batted his hand away. "I am fine now."

She carefully stepped toward the entrance and noted that the reflective stone was now covered with detritus. After crawling through the hole, the entrance turned abruptly to the right, and along the side was a dark, wide gap. The path itself was narrow by comparison, and the wall was irregular.

"I suggest we unload our supplies," Anna said quietly. Her voice echoed several times.

"I agree," Khal-Tral said. Anna could not see him in the darkness.

Anna crawled back out of the cave. Lamb was there with an arrow nocked watching the thicket where they had left their shufflers.

"Let us unload our equipment."

Chapter 20

?

The darkness beyond the entrance was unfathomable. Lamb had lit a torch, the stony gloom on all sides seeming to drink it. It was sufficient to illuminate the chasm enough to see Khan-Tral at the other end of the narrow ledge, where the path widened slightly.

"We are not going to be able to get the bulkier supplies past this," Anna said. She examined the walls. "I do not see any handholds, and who knows how deep that pit is."

"Perhaps we can set up a pulley system and send the supplies over that way?" Lamb said introspectively. "We just need something to slide along the rope."

"At the very least, the rope would give us something to hold on to," Anna replied. "The ledge is quite narrow in places."

"Khan-Tral," Lamb said quietly. They had established that whispered voices from Anna and Lamb could be heard clearly by the warrior, whereas he needed to shout to be heard.

"I AM HERE," the swordsman replied.

"I am going to shoot an arrow close to your position, and we will ferry the supplies across with it." The warrior grunted, which Lamb took as acknowledgment.

He adjusted the tension on the bow by turning the gears. Then, using one of the special arrowheads, Lamb wound half of one of the lengths of rope through the hole. When he was satisfied, he shot the arrow, which landed with a solid THUNK in the wall a few inches from Khan-Tral's head.

"A FINE SHOT, ARCHER!"

Anna and Lamb pulled on the other end of the rope as hard as they could to test the hold. It was solid. Lamb then drove another of the metal arrowheads into the wall on their side, and pulled the other end of the rope through it. He pulled it taut and tied the two ends together, leaving about ten feet of rope dangling.

"We can use that to tie bundles of supplies to the rope, and pull it to the other side where Khan-Tral can untie and stow it. Do you have space over there to put things?"

"THERE IS A SMALL CAVE ON THIS SIDE. IT SHOULD BE SUFFICIENT."

"Very well then," Anna said with satisfaction. "We should start with the saddle bags and do the bulkier things later."

"I don't know," Lamb replied. "Each time we put weight on the line, we risk pulling out the anchors. Perhaps we should send the heavier things first."

"It is a matter of what we can carry versus what we will need most," Anna countered.

"OK," Lamb conceded. Anna had already retrieved their saddle bags, so Lamb picked one set up and draped them over the rope. It sagged uncomfortably. "I don't know if it will hold the heavier things," he said to the swordsman. "We may have to leave them behind."

"WE WILL TAKE WHAT WE CAN," Khan-Tral replied. "THERE WAS NO GUARANTEE THAT ANYTHING WOULD FIT THROUGH THE NARROW SPACES WE MIGHT ENCOUNTER WITHIN."

Lamb shrugged and tied the saddle bags to one of the ropes. Then he started pulling the other and the bags drooped almost to the lip of the chasm before moving across.

"Oh my," Anna said, returning with their bedrolls. "I see your point, doctor."

"We'll have to make due," he said stoically.

◆

They had to tighten the ropes several times, but in the end, all of the supplies save for some kegs that worked loose and dropped endlessly into the chasm. Lamb tightened up the rope one more time before Anna took hold of it and steadied herself as she crossed the narrow ledge that was the path.

The going was slow as the height of the gap varied, but most of the way, she had to hunch forward precariously, putting her weight on the rope. She was about halfway down when the ropes suddenly bowed out, and Anna just barely managed to grip the ledge with her feet. Her body was fully extended, and she peered down blindly into the abyss.

"Are you hurt?" Lamb cried.

"I am fine," Anna replied, "but I do not think I can get back to the ledge without assistance."

"I'll come out to you," Lamb said quickly.

"STAY WHERE YOU ARE, ARCHER," Khan-Tral said from the opposite end of the ledge. Then, to Anna, "NYGOF, YOU MUST TAKE HOLD OF THE ROPE FIRMLY, FREE YOUR FEET, AND CLIMB THE REST OF THE WAY USING THE ROPE."

At the suggestion, Anna thought she would be afraid. But the space below was just as dark as the sections of the cave not illuminated by the lanterns at either end, so she had no feelings of vertigo or hesitation.

"Yes, Harry," she said with a strained, but even voice, "stay where you are. If you come to me, you will not have the rope for guidance." Lamb sighed, but remained in place.

Anna took a deep breath. Then she gripped the rope tightly with both hands and let her feet drop. The additional weight pulling on her arms was more than she had anticipated, and she cried out in alarm as the rope bit into her fingers.

"I'm coming!" Lamb shouted.

"No!" Anna commanded. "Do not risk yourself. I will manage. But put your gloves on before you head across." Anna had not imagined dangling from the rope, so she had not put her own gloves on. She winced against the pain, and pulled herself, hand over hand, across the gap beneath her. Her bloody fingers stained the rope as she progressed. When she was near the other side, her now-blood-coated hands slipped from the rope, but the warrior grabbed her and set her down beside him.

"IT IS NOW YOUR TURN, NAB."

Lamb pulled on the rope until the excess returned to his side. He tied the remainder of the rope around his waist. He silently chastised himself for not thinking of it before Anna had gone across. When he was ready, he followed Anna's example and inched down the ledge using the rope for balance. He managed to cross without incident.

"Well done," Khan-Tral said, slapping Lamb on the back while the doctor freed himself. He untied the ends of the rope and handed them to the warrior.

"Pull the rope back to us while I examine her hands," the doctor said. The swordsman took to his task.

Lamb kneeled next to Anna, who sat breathing heavily against the edge of the cavern. Using a cloth bandage from their supplies, and his water skin, he washed away the blood. There were numerous abrasions, but not of the wounds were deep.

"'Those are going to be raw for a while," the doctor said, "and we don't have any proper antiseptics. I'll wrap them, but keep your gloves on to help the wounds stay clean."

"I will do my best," Anna said with a weary smile. "For right now, I need to rest for a little while."

"A CAPITAL IDEA," the swordsman said, handing the coiled rope to Lamb. "I WILL SURVEY THE WAY AHEAD WHILE YOU TWO RESTORE YOURSELVES."

"Perhaps we should stay together-" Anna blurted out, but Khan-Tral was already gone.

◆

"How long do those burn for?" Anna asked, referring to their lantern. The one they had left on the opposite side of the chasm chamber had finally burned out.

"I think they should last for several days," Lamb replied, "but you need to adjust the wick every so often so it doesn't extinguish itself. And I don't think that one was filled completely." He examined the lamp that sat on the ground near them. "Khan-Tral must have filled this one to the top, because barely any oil has been used."

"Still," Anna continued, "Khan-Tral has been gone a long time. Perhaps we should see what has happened to him." She looked at the stack of bundles and kegs piled nearby. "But I don't think the two of us will be able to carry all of this."

"We'll take what we can," Lamb said in resignation. "But I want you to keep your hands free. Let those cuts and scrapes have time to heal."

"As you insist, doctor," Anna replied with mock seriousness.

They stood, and Lamb helped Anna put one of the loaded frames on her back.

"Is that too heavy?" he asked.

"It will get lighter as we go along," she replied with some effort.

Lamb sat and pulled the straps of another frame over his shoulders. But when he tried to stand, he could not get up. Anna grinned and pulled him to his feet. The doctor picked up one of the small kegs, which contained drinking water.

"We'll have to leave the rest here," he said, looking back at another loaded frame and half a dozen casks of water or lamp oil. "You take the lamp."

Anna picked up the lantern, glanced back at Lamb, and then stepped through the opening in the cave wall into a tunnel that was slightly taller than her and just wide enough to accommodate the loaded frame. The walls were fairly regular, and made of greenish stone with brownish layers throughout.

"It's a tight squeeze," Lamb said from behind her. "I can't get through carrying the keg. I'll have to leave it with the others."

Anna could not turn around in the cramped space, so she waited as she heard him put the keg down with a thud, followed by a rolling sound and the doctor's curses.

"One less keg to worry about," he said. "Went right over the edge, and I nearly knocked the others over after it!" He admonished himself quietly, but Anna could still hear him. Then a faint noise ahead of them caught her attention.

"I think that we should be quiet," she said quietly. "I expect that sounds travel very far in this narrow space. Listen!"

"That's Khan-Tral," Lamb said quietly, but with concern. Anna could discern his voice as well, though the words were muffled. They headed forward as quickly as the confined space and the light of the lantern allowed. Their gear rattled noisily against the frames and the walls.

The tunnel seemed to continue indefinitely. The uniform closeness of the walls becoming more oppressive with each step. Anna stopped when she could no longer keep up the pace and listened.

"What's wrong?" Lamb asked, also breathing heavily.

"I need to catch my breath," Anna said, "and I wanted to know if we can make out what is being said." She listened carefully, but did not hear anything. When her breathing had slowed, she started forward again. "Come on."

They continued down the narrow passage until it suddenly expanded into a cavern small enough to be almost fully illuminated by the lantern. The floor of the cave was covered with some kind of fungus, whose color was painful to look at. Lying in the center of the patch of fungus was Khan-Tral. His lantern lay on its side, and the contents of its fuel reservoir were puddled in a bare patch.

Chapter 21

?

Anna stepped into the cavern to allow Lamb to see. The doctor was about to run to the fallen man's side when Anna put out her arm to stop him from stepping on the fungus.

"There are spores floating in the air," she said. Lamb looked more carefully and noted the motes as they were illuminated by the torch. "I imagine that more were released when he stepped onto that growth."

"He may have been knocked out or asphyxiated by inhaling them," Lamb considered. Carefully, he took a light step onto the fungus. A small puff of spores were released by even that gentle touch. "I don't see a way around it."

Anna noted the broken torch, and the bare stone where the oil had pooled. "I think we can use the oil to kill the fungus," she said.

"We don't have a lot of it," Lamb replied, but he pulled a flask of lamp oil from Anna's frame, popped the cork, and poured a small amount on some of the fungus. To their astonishment, the growth seemed to retreat from the oil.

"At least we can make a path to him that way," Anna said. Lamb thought for a moment.

"What if we clear a space around him?" he said, and poured some more of the oil in a circle on the organism. The growth on the outside of the circle shied away from it, but what was trapped within turned brown and crumbled to dust. "That will work," the doctor said triumphantly. "You have six more flasks. What do I have on my frame?"

"You have six flasks as well," Anna replied after surveying Lamb's frame. "Let us see if we can make a perimeter around Khan-Tral using two or three."

"Better get two each," Lamb said, holding a pair flasks from her backpack. "Just in case." Anna retrieved two flasks from his frame. "Here goes."

The two poured the oil sparingly, creating a path to the fallen warrior. The growth retreated as expected. When they reached his body, they poured the oil in a circle around him, stepping where the fungus had already retreated. When they were finished, they had used all four bottles, and also spread the pooled oil from Khan-Tral's lantern. There was now a three-foot space around the body.

Lamb knelt beside the warrior and checked his pulse. The warrior was lying on his face. Lamb turned Khan-Tral's head to one side and felt for breath with his hand. The swordsman was breathing shallowly. The doctor wiped the encrusted dirt and spores from Khan-Tral's face with a wet cloth. A moment later, the warrior shuddered and attempted to rise.

"Hold on," Lamb said, gently holding him down. "You need to catch your breath and get some good air into your lungs."

In the meantime, Anna tried to examine the fungus more closely with her torch, but the matter retreated from the light. Using the cork of one of the empty oil flasks, she lit one end and quickly tossed the burning cork into the middle of the fungal growth. In a flash, the entire colony burst into flame and, just as quickly, the fire extinguished itself and the cavern floor was littered with the brown dust.

"Well done, Nygof" the warrior said weakly, catching his breath while extinguishing his eyebrows with his fingers. "We now know that the growth is highly flammable."

◆

While the warrior rested, Anna and Lamb took turns traversing the tunnel to retrieve the rest of their supplies.

"It's hard to get through the passages with a backpack while carrying a keg," Lamb advised.

"We will make due," the swordsman replied. "Also, the tunnels are not uniform. Some are much bigger than others." He looked up.

There were two other exits from the cavern. One appeared to be a continuation of the path they had been following. The other was a wider opening, perhaps five feet in diameter, in the ceiling.

"We need to go that way," Khan-Tral said. "It should lead to the floor of another cavern above. Shoot a line up and I will climb and see how far the next ledge is." As an afterthought, he added, "It might be beneficial to tie two of your ropes together."

Lamb considered the weight of the rope on the arrow, but in the end concluded that they did not really have a choice. While he made the preparations, Anna examined the mouth of the other tunnel.

"Are you sure we need to go up here?" she asked. "The tunnel we were traveling through seems to continue onward."

"There is a maze of tunnels down here," Khan-Tral said. "Some are empty rock, and others are inhabited by foul creatures, or worse, foul peoples."

"There are people living in the mountain?" Lamb asked incredulously.

"Indeed, Nab," the swordsman continued. "The denizens of the dark are as many and as varied as those on the surface. And the creatures have adapted to living in and among the rock."

"Are you saying that there are creatures that can move through the stone?" Now it was Anna's turn for amazement.

"Khan-Tral has seen the heads of beasts appear from within the solid rock, grab their prey, and pull it back into the stone with it leaving no sign of the breach." He glanced at Anna and Lamb. "The terrain is the least of our fears."

Lamb adjusted the tension on the box and shot a metal-tipped arrow up into the opening in the ceiling of the cavern. The coiled rope unwound rapidly. They heard the clink of the arrow striking something, and the rope hung limply a few feet off the ground.

"That is about a fifty- or sixty-foot climb," Lamb said skeptically.

"That is just where the arrow struck home," the warrior replied optimistically. "If Khan-Tral recalls correctly, the cavern ceiling above is some twenty or thirty feet high, so the climb will be that much less." He took the rope in both hands and pulled mightily, straining his muscles to test the arrow's hold.

"Khan-Tral will climb up and see the lay of the land." He grabbed the end of the rope with both hands, but just as he lifted himself off the ground the rope went slack, and a moment later the arrow clattered to the stone floor.

Lamb retrieved the arrow and examined it. The arrowhead was still sharp and pointy.

"It must not have had a good hold," Anna said. "Try again."

Lamb adjusted the tension on the mechanical bow almost to the maximum, nocked the arrow, and fired again. This time, the impact was much louder. Khan-Tral pulled on the rope using all his strength, and then test-climbed up a few feet.

"This is much more secure, Nab," he said with a smile. "I will be back shortly."

◆

Some time later, there was a tug on the rope. Anna and Lamb debated what it meant.

"SEND UP MY GEAR," a distant voice said from above. Lamb tied Khan-Tral's frame securely to the end of the rope and tugged on it. The frame ascended. A short while later, a light appeared in the shaft above them, illuminating almost all of it. It narrowed slightly after the initial opening, but was fairly wide.

"THERE IS A WIDE LEDGE HERE. WE CAN BRING OUR EQUIPMENT HERE AND THEN CLIMB FARTHER."

"That sounds wise," Anna said in amusement. "We do not want to leave it unattended if these caverns are occupied as he suggested."

"I suppose," Lamb said. He examined Anna's hands and noted that the wrappings were blood-stained. "I'll do it. You rest those hands. I'll replace the bandages after we climb up there."

"As you wish," Anna said. "I will keep watch."

Lamb tied the next frame to the rope when it reappeared and tugged again. The operation went smoothly, and everything was borne up to the swordsman in no time.

"You go next," Lamb said. He took hold of the end of the rope to steady it.

"Very well." Anna grabbed the rope with both hands and pulled herself up. The grip was painful, but she kept her discomfort to herself. She made slow progress, and once clear of the doctor, wrapped her legs around it as well.

When she reached the entrance to the shaft, Anna put her back against one side and wedged herself in place with her feet across the gap.

"IS ALL WELL?" Khan-Tral said from above.

"I am fine," she replied. "Just resting my hands."

"Try walking up the shaft," Lamb suggested. "That may take the strain off your hands."

"I was thinking the same thing," she said.

Carefully, Anna took hold of the rope again. She gripped it tightly, then stretched her back up the shaft until her legs were nearly extended. Then she slowly walked up the other side of the gap one foot at a time. She continued in this manner until Khan-Tral's strong arms engulfed her from behind and lifted her onto the ledge.

"You did well," he said with a smile. "Khan-Tral is impressed by your ingenuity." Anna was not sure of the muscle-bound swordsman was being supportive or condescending. She elected to believe he was being positive. She grinned as she considered whether or not he knew how to be condescending.

◆

Anna considered her persona in this world. Nygof was known as a spy and assassin. She allegedly had skill with knives and axes, and was known for her stealth. Her reputation had impaired the well-being of "her family." But she was not universally reviled. The Draunskur, who were followers of Utgarda, seemed to be friendly toward her.

Sif was hostile, but that was because she knew who Anna really was and held her responsible for her transformation into that insect queen. Ganon and Govil followed Sif blindly, so their hostility had also been justified, though Ganon had seemed to be friendlier.

A flash of realization appeared in Anna's mind. A memory she had misplaced somehow. It seemed that all her allies, according to Brian Teplow, were now adversaries. Ganon had certainly been helpful in New York. Govil had been Arthur Coffin, the detective sent by Utgarda to thwart their attempts to dispel the demon. But Coffin had turned out to be the key to their success.

Liv Lee had been infatuated with Lamb from the moment the two met, and Queen Sif, her alter ego, seemed enamored with him initially. Anna had only met her the one time in her apartment, and the negative impression Lee had had of Anna had carried forward to Lee's current incarnation.

Anna thought that Khan-Tral, Peter Gulden in the real world, had been an adversary. He had set her up be killed in what would look like a gangland shooting. But now he was their biggest ally.

What did that imply about Deb-Roh and Gho-Bazh?

Lamb emerged from the hole a short time later. Anna that Nab had noted that this version of the doctor was quite skillful, both with the bow as well as with tracking and climbing. She imagined that this persona must be a successful hunter under normal conditions.

Chapter 22

?

The three rested and ate some of their rations. The rope climbed even farther into the darkness above them, so they wanted to be refreshed before moving onward.

In the continuous darkness, it was impossible to measure time. Anna had no idea how long they had been traversing the passages, but they had entered the catacombs in mid-afternoon. By her reckoning, it must be late evening by now.

"It's going to take time for those to heal," Lamb said. "And all this climbing won't help." Lamb had changed the wrappings for clean ones, dropping the blood-stained rags down the shaft.

Anna's muscles ached, and her palms burned. Sitting on the ledge had only caused her back, arms, and legs to stiffen up, and she realized how tired she was.

"Perhaps we should get some sleep," she suggested. Lamb yawned in agreement however Khan-Tral seemed unaffected.

"If you require rest," he said, and again Anna could not tell if he was being supportive or condescending, "Khan-Tral will keep watch. We should be safe enough here."

Something in his response concerned Anna, but she was too tired to give it much thought. Lamb had unconsciously sat down and snuggled up against her, and Anna suddenly realized that his head now rested on her shoulder. They had gotten into the habit of sleeping close to each other for warmth, so she did not give it a second thought.

◆

Anna awakened with a start, Lamb's hand over her mouth. She nodded recognition, and he released her.

"Khan-Tral heard movement above us," he said quietly. "He's gone up to investigate." The rope twitched as the warrior climbed. It seemed like an eternity before he climbed back down again.

"There are signs of something very large being slid across the floor," the swordsman said quietly, "but Khan-Tral did not see anything in the cavern above."

"How far up is the opening?" Lamb asked.

"Not far. We have climbed more than halfway. The cavern itself is quite large. There is a primary tunnel passing through it that we want to take, as well as two other side passages and another in the ceiling."

"What do you think you heard?" Anna asked.

"It sounded like something being slid across the ground," the warrior replied. "And that agrees with the marks Khan-Tral found on the floor. But they did not go very far, nor did they seem to go anywhere in particular."

"We should proceed with caution then," Lamb said.

Khan-Tral nodded, grabbed a lantern and took it by the handle in his teeth, and immediately climbed back up the rope.

"I didn't mean right now-" he added, but the warrior had already disappeared into the blackness. A moment later, light appeared about ten feet above them. "I guess it's time to go."

◆

As before, Anna walked up the narrow shaft, and then Khan-Tral pulled up the supplies.

While this was happening, Anna lit another lantern and explored the illuminated part of the cavern. It was significantly larger than any of the previous chambers, and the walls were grey with white flecks here and there. There was what appeared to be a main thoroughfare passing through the chamber. The tunnels on opposite sides of the cave were tall and arched, easily big enough to pull a wagon through. The two other tunnels were smaller and more natural-looking. She could not see the alleged shaft in the ceiling.

Anna realized that the cavern, despite its size, was fairly clean. The ever-present dust was significantly lessened, making the wide track through it barely visible. It was nearly ten feet across and seemed to go haphazardly around the space, stopping at the foot of an enormous stalagmite.

Anna turned to see Lamb poke out from the hole in the floor and gasp.

DESTROY IT, a voice said in his head.

◆

O'Malley jumped as three Junazhi appeared at his side, the stalks on their heads, and on Bierce's attachment, flashing rapidly.

"What's going on?" he cried. Then he looked back at the image and shuddered. Anna stood next to a giant, conical being with twin stalks like a slug near the point. As he watched, numerous, ropey tentacles emerged seamlessly from orifices in its surface and reached for her.

◆

"LOOK OUT," Khan-Tral cried, leaping toward Anna, his huge sword at the ready.

Anna saw Lamb fire half a dozen arrows in rapid succession and the swordsman charge toward her, Nightbane at the ready. She looked up and behind her where the others seemed be focusing and saw the tentacles coming for her. Instinctively, she pulled two knives from her bandoleer and rolled away from the oncoming appendages.

Khan-Tral arrived a moment later and sliced through the tentacles just before they reached her. Lamb's arrows barely missed one of the stalks, which evaded them effortlessly.

◆

DESTROY IT, O'Malley heard a voice say in his head. The Junazhi stalks continued to flash furiously. A moment later, Lamb shot off a series of arrows.

"The Junazhi can communicate with them!" O'Malley shouted.

"**Not now**," Bierce replied. "**That is one of the Junazhi's ancient enemies.**"

"What is it doing in Brian Teplow's dream world?"

"**That is a good question. I suspect that, just as the Junazhi can impose themselves into it, the ancient enemy can do so as well.**"

YOU CANNOT DEFEAT ME, another voice said loudly in his head. O'Malley covered his ears, but it did nothing to reduce the volume. *YOUR PUPPETS ARE POWERLESS. THE DARK ONE WILL BE DEFEATED.*

◆

Anna fought desperately to hold off the tentacles, but they kept coming. While her knives bit into them, they could not slice through, and the wounds closed almost instantly. Even Khan-Tral's sword only provided a temporary respite. The severed ends pursued them as the limbs regenerated and attacked again a moment later.

Suddenly, the colossal thing slid toward them at surprising speed. Anna and Khan-Tral dove out of the way in opposite directions.

Lamb kept firing as he ran toward Anna. His arrows stuck the mass of the thing and seemed to disappear harmlessly into it.

The mass stopped when the Razor of Delusions sliced into it from the other side. Lamb fired off several more shots, striking the thing squarely in the center. This time, they seemed to have some effect.

Instead of closing, a gelatinous green goo erupted from the wound and pooled on the floor. As they watched, the mass expanded rapidly, and countless mouths, eyes, and pseudopods appeared.

"RUN," Khan-Tral cried as he sprinted into view around the conical creature. He was heading toward the passage nearest Anna and Lamb, which was one of the smaller, natural ones. Anna turned to follow.

Lamb shot an arrow at the globular monster slurping toward him, but the shaft disintegrated as soon as it made contact. Lamb turned and followed the others as fast as he could.

◆

"What does it mean 'the Dark One will be defeated,'" O'Malley shouted at Bierce. "Who is the enemy here? Or are all of these things to be vanquished?" He brandished the relic defensively in case someone or something attacked him. But nothing threatened him.

"As you can well imagine," Bierce said, "the Junazhi have their own long and storied history. Their story precedes the concept of humanity or life as you know it. From their perspective, as well as that of their ancient enemy, humanity is inconsequential. The 'Dark One' it spoke of could be anything."

O'Malley considered this. These entities all seemed to transcend space and time. Contrary to theological dogma, in the grand scheme of the universe, the existence of mankind or even life on Earth is inconsequential. Still, he was skeptical of the aliens' motives.

◆

Khan-Tral led the three through the tunnel. There was light up ahead. After about twenty feet, it opened up into a tall chamber dominated by a stalagmite that reached up toward with a stalactite. The two were connected by few feet of ice on a narrow ledge.

Emerging from the tunnel, Lamb looked back and watched the light from their abandoned lantern disappear as the monster filled the passage behind them. Fortunately, it did not seem to move very quickly.

"Up top," he shouted and started climbing the stalagmite. Anna and Khal-Tral followed suit. They could hear the sound of the creature as got closer, preceded by a noxious cloud that caused their noses to burn and their eyes to water.

The stalagmite was pitted and the climbing was fairly easy, even for Anna. When they reached the top, Anna realized that the ice between the stalagmite and the stalactite was glowing. It illuminated the chamber.

As Khan-Tral helped Lamb onto the surface, the monster emerged from the tunnel. To their horror, it continued to grow, expanding like rising dough, coming closer and closer.

Like a moth to a flame, Anna reached out and touched the glowing ice. The was a flash, and then she was gone. Lamb and Khan-Tral saw her disappear, touched the ice themselves, and disappeared as well.

Chapter 23

July 17, 1929

"You still have not explained to me how they can communicate with Harry," O'Malley said with irritation. The Junazhi vanished as soon as the image on the screen went blank. The priest kept the relic at the ready, but there were no targets.

He turned with a start and nearly blasted Billy, but the silent watchmen was merely setting a tray of sandwiches with a pot of coffee and a single mug on the table next to the Bierce device.

"I take it with cream and sugar," O'Malley said sarcastically. Billy turned the tray to reveal a sugar bowl and small pitcher, which had been hidden by the pot. "Thank you," he said apologetically out of habit.

"I mentioned previously that the Junazhi sense things differently from you," Bierce said. "They can communicate telepathically to Dr. Lamb. It appears to him as a compelling thought. He does not even realize it."

"So he was the puppet that cone thing referred to," O'Malley fumed. "And they can command him at will to do their bidding without him even realizing it? What else have they had him do?"

"You have been present since his implantation. They have not sent him any instructions other than to attack the ancient enemy. And that, I assure you, was an instinct burned into their collective memory."

"So you're saying that making Harry fire at that thing was an involuntary reaction to seeing it."

"That is correct."

"So these aliens have things that go bump in the night too." O'Malley considered that information. He noticed Billy move to stand behind him, an arm's reach away. "Interesting."

◆

Anna awoke with a start and started rolling on the ground. She felt as if she was on fire, but realized that the glowing, metallic square that she and her companions were laying upon was extremely hot, and only their clothes had shielded them from burning. She rolled off the square, which was elevated about a foot over the soft floor of a vast cavern, and rose to her knees.

"WAKE UP!" she shouted, reaching out to shake Lamb's leg. The doctor stirred, and then duplicated Anna's previous movements, including shaking Khan-Tral awake. The swordsmen leapt from a lying position off the platform and landed on his feet behind the other two.

Anna looked around the cavern, which appeared to be illuminated by some kind of phosphorescent fungus growing all around. The cavern was enormous. They could see neither the sides nor the ceiling. The metal platform stood in the center of a thick, subterranean forest. A few feet back from the heat of the platform, a thick carpet of moss-like growth covered the ground. Here and there, large mushrooms grew as big as trees.

Lamb gazed in wonder at the plant life all around. He heard the trickle of water and followed the sound. It emanated from a small brook that pooled into a pond. As he approached, Lamb noted the rustling of the foliage, suggesting that something or things had fled his approach. He knelt by the water and unconsciously took a drink. The water tasted cool and fresh.

Suddenly, he saw a large shape move rapidly in the water and stepped back as a four- or five-foot pike-like fish leapt from the water and snapped at where he had been, before disappearing back below the surface. Lamb backtracked to where he had left the others, only to emerge on the opposite side of the platform from them.

"Where are we?" Anna asked, amazed at the beauty of the underground garden.

"Khan-Tral is not sure," the swordsman said with uncharacteristic uncertainty. "He would surely remember growth such as this. Khan-Tral does not believe that he has been here before."

"So we're lost?!" Lamb cried. "How are we supposed to find Brian now? We'll wander these tunnels forever before we stumble upon an exit."

"Not necessarily," Anna said, examining the mushroom trees. "Mushroom such as these require consistent temperature and moisture. This cavern is comparatively warmer than those below, which suggests that it is closer to the surface."

"Unless there is some other heat source down here," Lamb retorted. "I read somewhere that caves tend to be a uniform temperature, around 52 degrees Fahrenheit. There must be some other source for the additional warmth."

"Regardless of the cause of the growth here," Khan-Tral interjected, "a forest such as this is likely to be inhabited, so be wary. Subterranean predators can be more cunning than their surface counterparts."

"Our first priority is to assess our situation," Anna said in a fresh, business-like manner. "We have lost all of our supplies except what we have with us. Therefore we have no food, water, lanterns, or oil."

"There is a pond over there," Lamb said, pointing over his shoulder with his thumb, "but we have nothing to carry the water in. I drank some. It's fresh."

"How cold was the water?" the swordsman asked curiously.

"How cold?" Lamb asked. "I don't know. It hadn't just thawed from ice, if that's what you mean. What does it matter?"

The warrior did not respond, but instead stepped purposefully into the foliage, where all but his head and shoulders disappeared. As they watched, he looked from side to side and up and down as if searching for something.

"We had better stay together," Anna said and followed the trail of trampled vegetation. Lamb followed with an arrow nocked, watching their rear.

◆

They followed Khan-Tral in silence for some time. They had given up asking him to explain himself a while ago after repeated shushing. When the cavern wall came into view, the swordsman seemed disconcerted. He tracked the wall to his right and Anna followed his gaze, but Lamb looked the other way.

"What's that?" the doctor said, pointing to a narrow strip running up the side of the cavern in the distance. Khan-Tral turned, saw the subject of his inquiry, and smiled.

"You've found it. Khan-Tral knows where we are, and we are much closer to our goal."

"What is that?" Anna asked.

"That," he said with a grin, "is a ladder hammered into the side of the cavern. There is a trapdoor in the cavern roof at the top that will put us one layer below Gho-Bazh's dungeon."

"Who put it there?" Lamb asked.

"Khan-Tral does not know, but it was there when he and Deb-Roh made their escape. Come!"

The warrior led Anna and Lamb along the wall of the cavern until they came upon another pool along the edge. Avoiding the water, they stepped back into the thick foliage.

Suddenly, something leapt onto Lamb and knocked him out of view.

Anna heard the commotion behind her and turned to see that Lamb was missing. She heard a commotion in the growth to her left, drew twin hand axes from her bandoleer, and dove in.

What she found was a growling mass of fur with sharp claws. She caught a glimpse of a rodent-like snout and a long, furry tail, but it darted through the underbrush too fast to properly recognize.

Lamb was trying to fend off the creature, but the dense foliage was too thick for him to draw his sword. He had fallen into a sitting position, and the mass of fur and fury seemed to circle around him continuously.

Anna tried to reach in and attack, but she was fearful of hitting the doctor.

Then Khan-Tral was at her side. He reached in and took hold of the creature. The greyish-brown fur consolidated into a large, weasel-like creature. The swordsman gripped it in both hands behind its forelimbs, but the creature had sufficient mobility to wrap its long body and tail around one of his arms and claw at it.

Anna took her chance and chopped at the creature's head with her axe. She missed, striking the swordsman's belt buckle instead.

The creature paused for a moment to assess the new attacker, and Anna lashed out with the other axe, landing a solid chop across the back of its neck. The animal screeched, but had lost most of its mobility. She chopped again and the neck broke with a solid crunch.

Anna dropped the axes and knelt at Lamb's side. "Are you hurt?"

Lamb looked himself over. His long sleeves and trousers had been torn in several places, and there were some scratches on his hands and face, but he did not detect anything more than superficial injuries.

"I don't believe there is anything life threatening," he replied, "as long as that weasel didn't have rabies. But we'll have to take our chances."

Anna helped him to his feet and then retrieved her axes. When they returned to the trail Khan-Tral had blazed, she noticed that the warrior had the giant weasel's headless corpse draped over his shoulders.

"A memento?" she asked.

"This will make a fine coat," the swordsman replied and trekked forward into the fungus forest.

Chapter 24

?

By the time they had circumvented the pond, the direct path seemed much closer than returning to the cavern wall, so they continued on through the mushrooms and moss until they discovered a road of stone-grey brick that passed from an opening in one wall, through the cavern, and out another opening on the opposite side, barely visible in the distance. The road was wide enough for two-way traffic, and ruts in the bricks indicated use by heavy carts or wagons.

Khan-Tral knelt and examined the tracks and the brickwork.

"Come quickly," he said abruptly as he suddenly rose and advanced toward the ladder, unconcerned with the terrain between them and it.

"What is it?" Anna asked, jogging to keep up with him and tripping on the occasional vine.

"There are beings that live below the ground," the warrior said gravely. "Things that see anything not like them as food or slaves. We want to avoid them if we can." As an afterthought, he added, "That is why no one else has escaped the Red Wizard this way."

"What kind of things?" Lamb asked.

"Let us hope that you do not find out," Khan-Tral said ominously, his pace never slowing.

Eventually the foliage gave way to open ground. The ever-present moss ended just short of the wall. Anna saw the iron ladder, which was mounted in the rock of the cavern wall about one foot out from the face and rose perhaps 100 feet to a metal door that could barely be discerned in the ceiling.

Khan-Tral stepped out into the clearing, followed by Anna and Lamb. They were crossing the moss when suddenly a net shot out from concealment and engulfed them. The weighted strands pulled them to the ground as a horn trumpeted before dying out, as if a bladder of air had been exhausted.

While Khan-Tral pulled at the heavy ropework with his bare hands, Lamb set to cutting the net with an arrowhead. Anna was able to draw the knives from her wrist sheathes. Her razor-sharp blades sliced through the web of strands easily, and in a moment, she was out of the net and cutting out Lamb.

The sound of armored feet running across the stone caught their ears, echoing from the nearer roadway tunnels, and an aura of apprehension overcame Anna. The warrior noticed her discomfort.

"Quickly!" Khan-Tral said. "The Druegar are coming!"

Anna freed Lamb, who nocked an arrow and watched toward where the sound was coming from. He could not see the tunnel mouth beyond the foliage, so it was likely that whoever was coming would not be able to see them.

Suddenly he was lifted from behind by Khan-Tral and thrust up onto the ladder. Anna was already quickly climbing ahead of him. He followed, and the warrior brought up the rear as soon as he was clear.

As she crested the top of the mushroom trees, Anna hazarded a glance back toward where the noise was coming from. As she watched, a half a dozen short, bald, wide men dressed in chainmail armor emerged from the tunnel. They immediately looked in her direction and ran toward the ladder.

Behind them, a couple more appeared leading a train of humanoid beings, but clearly not all human, who were mostly naked, and shackled together by the neck with their arms chained behind them. The latter ones poked and prodded the captives with their spears.

"KEEP GOING!" Khan-Tral shouted up to Anna. "THE DRUEGAR CAN'T CLIMB THE LADDER. THEY'RE TOO HEAVY! ONCE WE'RE HIGH ENOUGH, WE'RE CLEAR!"

Anna renewed her efforts and advanced rapidly up the ladder. Lamb followed, but he was not as confident on the ladder and his feet kept slipping off the rungs. He jumped when arrows started striking the walls around them. The Druegar were not good shots, but it would only take one stray shot.

An arrow struck the rung Lamb was about to grab and pulled his attention away. His foot slipped and his other hand gave way. He struck the ladder and flipped over, falling face-first. But Khan-Tral caught his leg is his meaty fist.

"I'VE GOT YOU," he said, clearly strained. "GRAB THE LADDER WHEN YOU CAN."

◆

O'Malley turned away when Lamb lost his grip on the ladder. He turned back to see the floor of the cavern, perhaps twenty feet below. Harry was hanging upside down. Lamb looked out into the cavern and saw about a dozen armored dwarves running toward him. They stopped every few steps to fire a volley of arrows.

"Get climbing, Harry," O'Malley said in desperation.

"He cannot hear you."

"I know!" the priest snapped back. "It just helps me feel less impotent," he added quietly.

◆

Lamb hung upside down perhaps 20 feet above the Druegar. Helplessly, he reached out to catch the contents of his quiver as they dropped past, soothed only by the fact that the heavy metal arrowheads pointed downward when they struck those below. However, only a single arrow hit one of the armored figures, and it bounced harmlessly off his helmet.

Fear and desperation filled him. At the last moment, he was able to catch the ornate, golden baton that he had found among the Draunskur horde, which had gotten caught in the fabric of the quiver. He gripped the baton hard as a spasm of pain erupted from the leg Khan-Tral was tightly gripping. A blue bolt of energy shot from the device and blasted away a section of the cavern floor in a blinding flash.

When his vision cleared, Lamb saw four of the small warriors on the ground, blackened and smoking, while their peers retreated to the concealment of the foliage.

"Good shot, archer," Khan-Tral said with some effort, "but take hold of the ladder now. Khan-Tral is losing his grip."

Lamb reached out and grabbed the ladder with both hands, and then looped his free leg around one of the higher rungs.

"You should have led with that," the warrior said with humor in his voice.

"I didn't know it could do that," the doctor replied. "Now help me get right-side-up!" He felt the ladder shake as the warrior descended. A moment later, Lamb was lifted by his belt and pulled from the ladder. He nearly dropped the baton. He rose slightly, until he was almost level with the warrior, who had looped his own arm around a rung and now lifted Lamb over his head.

"Take hold of the rungs with your hands reversed," the warrior said. Lamb followed his instructions and was quickly ascending the ladder between Anna and Khan-Tral.

◆

Anna had not stopped climbing. She was preoccupied with the ladder and reaching the top. The nervous tension the aggressors seemed to radiate remained strong. Also, she knew not to look down from a height, as it might cause vertigo.

She climbed steadily. Her arms ached and each rung irritated her bandaged hands, but adrenaline kept her going. Eventually, she reached the top of the ladder, where a metal hatch was built into the stone ceiling. Anna pushed on the hatch with her shoulder, but it did not move.

As she pondered, her fatigue caught up with her. Instinctively, she stepped down a rung, put her legs though the ladder, and sat precariously on the metal step.

She examined the edges and could not see how the door opened. There were no evident hinges, and any handle seemed to be on the other side. Perhaps this was the bottom of a trapdoor. But then why would there be a ladder up to it from below?

Anna's musings were interrupted when something tapped her bottom. She was too tired to react, and peered down to see Lamb looking up at her, with Khan-Tral right behind him. The doctor was holding an ornate, golden baton of the style given to commanders of Roman legions. It glowed slightly, and Anna could feel residual heat emanating from it.

"Comfortable?" Lamb said with amusement, though his strain and fatigue was evident. The glowing baton illuminated the hatch, and Anna noted characters engraved in it. She peered closer, but her head cast a shadow over them.

"Lend me your staff," she said to Lamb, holding out a hand behind her. She felt the warm metal in her palm. The heat was unexpectedly soothing on the wounds. She brought the light closer to the characters, but they were partially encrusted with grime. She wiped away the grit, and it exposed an indentation.

Anna moved the baton closer to examine the interior of the indentation, and when it got within an inch of the space the end of the golden rod was sucked into the gap as if magnetically, and there was a hiss. The baton was released from the hatch, and Anna pulled it out. Then the panel rose slightly and slid to the side into the ceiling of the cavern.

Beyond the exposed portal was a shaft of perhaps another ten feet. A similar ladder continued up the opening.

"There is another-" Anna started to say.

"Just keep going!" Lamb shouted. "I can't hold on much longer!"

Without hesitation, Anna lowered the baton and dropped it carefully into Lamb's open-topped quiver. Then she continued climbing.

When the three were all climbing the second ladder, the hatch below slid closed on its own. Anna continued climbing and discovered that the shaft from which she emerged had been covered by a leathery animal skin. Beyond it was a cavern littered with rubble from fallen stalactites and the mounds of broken stalagmites.

"What was that?" she heard a quiet voice say, followed by a shushing sound.

Anna quietly attempted to cover the opening again. The animal skin was stiff enough to be moved from beneath, but she had no idea if moving it had made it visible from above. Then she climbed down to Lamb.

"There is a cavern beyond that cover, but I heard someone sneaking around inside it. They did not want to be discovered."

"We are at their mercy down here," Khan-Tral said from below. "We must get on an equal footing, whether they be friend or foe."

"Is there cover or anything?" Lamb asked.

"There are many broken stalactites and stalagmites strewn about, but I did not get that good a look." She pictured the room in her mind. "There is a mound about three feet high and perhaps five feet wide a couple feet to the left of the opening. The voices I heard were to the right. Head for that mound as quietly as you can."

With the silent consent of the others, Anna climbed back up. She quietly lifted the animal skin barely off the ground and folded it over itself to the right. Then she peered out in the direction from which she had heard the noise.

"We don't know what that was," she heard a different voice whisper. "Best to stay hidden until it reveals itself."

"I'm scared," the first voice whined, and Anna heard a gentle tapping sound. She stifled a chuckle and pointed in the direction of the sound.

Climbing out of the hole, Anna quietly stepped through a layer of dust and hid behind the indicated rock. She peered around to watch Lamb emerge, look around, and freeze. He scanned the cave warily and caught sight of Anna, who motioned him toward her urgently.

Lamb crawled awkwardly out of the hole. The rustling was evident. Lamb recovered and loped toward Anna, but as she watched where the sounds had come from she saw two disheveled men, one bearded and one younger, peer around a similar outcropping. The older one saw Lamb and ducked back down, grabbing the other one's shirt. As he fell, the latter made eye contact with Anna.

Khan-Tral vaulted from the hole, glanced at Anna, and then leapt over the rock she was looking at. A moment later, the giant warrior lifted the two off the ground by the collars of their garments.

Chapter 25

?

"WHO WOULD SEEK TO WAYLAY KHAN-TRAL AND HIS COMPANIONS?" the warrior shouted.

"Please don't hurt us, my lord," the bearded man whispered, "and please lower your voice. We are right below the dungeons of the Red Wizard, Gho-Bazh!"

"Khan-Tral?" the younger one said quietly with evident excitement. "They said you would return. They said you would come back for Deb-Roh. Finally the Red Wizard will be defeated."

"You know of Khan-Tral and Deb-Roh?" Anna said as she emerged from her hiding place. "Who told you about them?"

"Everybody knows the story of Khan-Tral and Deb-Roh," the younger one said proudly. "The warrior and the scout, traveling all the lands righting wrongs and fighting for the oppressed."

"Your story is common knowledge where we come from," the older added.

"What more is said of them?" Lamb asked, standing beside Anna. "How do the stories say the Red Wizard will be defeated?"

"Why, Khan-Tral will summon an army from the stars and lay siege to Gho-Bazh's palace," the older one said. "The Red Wizard will challenge Khan-Tral to single combat," he looked side to side furtively, "but he will cheat. He will have archers waiting in concealment to kill the warrior when he emerges into the arena."

"How does Khan-Tral prevail?" Anna asked.

"Unknown to the Red Wizard," the younger one said, "Khan-Tral recruited assassins of his own, who silently dispatch Gho-Bazh's archers. When the sneak attack fails to happen, the wizard is distracted, and the mighty swordsman chops off his head."

"And this story is common knowledge," Lamb asked, "even among the Red Wizard's guards and household?

"Yes, my lord," the younger one replied. "That story has been unchanged for generations."

"It was passed from my father to me," the older one corrected sheepishly, "and I told it to my son here exactly as I remembered it."

Khan-Tral returned the two to the ground and released their collars. The younger one looked Anna up and down, and then excitement bloomed in his eyes.

"You're Nygof," he shouted, then caught himself and whispered, "the Shadow!" He beamed. "Gho-Bazh doesn't have a chance now!"

"There are still many challenges to be overcome before we can strike at the Red Wizard," Khan-Tral said. "To begin with, the terrain is much changed from what Khan-Tral recalls. He needs you to tell him the lay of the land."

"How did you come to be here?" Anna asked.

"We were in a cell in the dungeon," the young man said. "The Red Wizard captured our whole village and brought everyone back to his castle."

"Why?" Anna asked.

"To sacrifice to the Other Gods to keep the Dark One trapped here," the older one replied. Anna and Lamb exchanged unhappy glances.

"As I was saying," the younger one continued, "the three of us were in a cell, and he heard horrible noises coming from a door at the end of the hall."

"Screams and death wails," the older one chimed in, "like people being tortured."

"So we were trapped in that cell," the younger one started choking up, "and they came-"

"And they came for my wife," the old man said. "We fought them, but they threw me to the floor and took her away."

"We heard her scream in agony for hours-" the younger one said and then sat weeping.

"So I was determined not to let that fate happen to my boy. I checked all the cracks in the walls looking for loose stones or cracks I could expand and such, and I found an outline in the floor. I blew away the dust and there was a seam all around it. Together, we managed to pry it up, but it was real heavy."

"There was a tunnel beneath it. So we climbs down and down and finds a cave. There's a tunnel from the cave, and we ended up here."

"They must have been in the same cell as Khan-Tral and Deb-Roh," the warrior said with a grin. "The tunnel is still there." He glanced toward a low side tunnel on the wall facing them.

"Did you cover the hole back up?" Anna asked urgently. The two looked sheepish.

"Well, "the older one said, "no. We was focused on escaping. We went down and didn't look back."

"Then your escape has probably been discovered by now," Lamb said in frustration.

"I don't think so," the older one said. "It took a long time to pry out that stone, and we were never looked in on. I don't think there's any guards in the dungeon now."

"I heard some of them talking about a campaign in the Endless Barrens of None to take the fight to the Dark One," the younger one said. "That was about the time Father found the entrance. A short time after that, they stopped bringing us food, and then stopped coming by at all."

"I saw Gho-Bazh and an army crossing the Endless Barrens by air just a few days ago," Anna told Khan-Tral.

"Even if he knew who we were and where we were going," Lamb conjectured, "I imagine it would take several days to return to his palace from there."

"Yes, my lord," the older one said. "Our village was on the border of the Endless Barrens, and it took us a week to walk here in chains."

"Indeed," the younger one added, "and even without the burden of prisoners, it would still take a few days."

"You have been most helpful," Khan-Tral said with a smile, and patted the two on the back. "What is your plan now?" The pair looked at each other.

"We don't have a plan, my lord," the older one said. "Perhaps it would be best to stay with you."

"I am afraid that we cannot risk bringing you with us," Anna said evenly. The two escapees looked at her, wide-eyed.

"We don't have any supplies to share with you," Lamb said, "but I advise you not to go down that shaft."

"If memory serves," Khan-Tral said, "and I may be mistaken - I don't recall all this debris - there should be a passage that way. Follow that tunnel until you get to a cavern with an entrance that has been carved to look like some kind of beast. In that cavern, you will find a concealed exit in the floor bearing stairs. That is the route that Khan-Tral and Deb-Roh used to flee this place."

"Thank you, my lord," the old man said, bowing low, first to Khan-Tral, then to Anna, and finally to Lamb.

The young one was overwhelmed by the experience. He glanced from Khan-Tral to Anna to Lamb and back to Anna, and then hugged her tightly. She broke the embrace violently. The man dropped to his knees and looked up at her begging.

"I'm sorry," he said. "I don't know what came over me." Anna softened and extended her hand to help him to his feet.

"You have been through a lot," she said, "so I forgive you." He moved to embrace her again, but she raised a finger to stop him and shook her head. He stepped back and nodded respectfully.

"Go now," Khan-Tral said, "but be wary. This underground realm is perilous beyond your imagination." As they turned to go, Anna handed each of them one of her two hand axes.

"You will need these," she said, and then turned toward the tunnel to the Red Wizard's dungeons.

◆

Anna examined the indicated tunnel. It was dark, and looked natural. She noted faint light about thirty feet down the passage. The tunnel was barely big enough to crawl through, and she wondered how Khan-Tral had managed to the first time.

"From this point forward," the warrior whispered from behind, catching Anna by surprise, "we should proceed as quietly and carefully as we can." He paused for Anna and Lamb to indicate understanding. "Beyond this tunnel, excavated by Khan-Tral and Deb-Roh, are the cells of Gho-Bazh, where unfortunates are held for the Red Wizard's vile rituals."

Lamb considered the tunnel and wondered what had happened to the displaced dirt, but the others entered the passage before he could ask. Up close, it was evident that the walls and sides were composed of packed earth, and there was evidence of work by bare hands. But it was curious that the was earth suitable for digging here rather than stone. The thought nagged at him, but he hurried to keep up.

Anna was surprised when the warrior's head bumped into her bottom. The large man was evidently quite capable of traversing the narrow passage. She quickened her pace as much as she thought she could while still remaining quiet, but she once again felt the impact on her rear. At first she thought the swordsman was being forward, but this was neither the time or the place for such thoughts.

The tunnel opened up on a slightly wider space. The light came from an opening perhaps eight feet above, accessed by a hand-dug shaft. The space was wide enough for Anna, but once Khan-Tral entered, it became quite cramped. Silently and effortlessly, the warrior lifted Anna by her legs and thrust her up the shaft.

The room above was a cell. A simple stone cube with a heavy, reinforced wooden door. There was a small grill in the doorway that revealed nothing but darkness beyond.

Anna pulled herself up and into the cell. Khan-Tral emerged almost immediately. He laid on the floor and ducked his head, arms, and torso into the hole, returning holding Lamb by both wrists. He set the doctor down on the floor and all three sat against the wall next to the door so as not to be seen by passers-by.

Anna listened carefully. She could hear creaks and drips, but no signs of life. There were no cries or groans of prisoners. No clink of keys or armor. No taps of spears on the ground. No sounds one would expect in a dungeon.

She looked to the others and put her hand to her ear and shook her head. Lamb nodded acknowledgment, but Khan-Tral stood and looked out the window in the door. He turned to the other two, walked his across his palm, and shook his head. Then he put his head against the wood of the door and leaned into it, listening intently.

The swordsman smiled and motioned for Anna to join him. She stood, and Lamb followed. Khan-Tral pointed a finger at the keyhole in the door and made a turning motion.

Anna looked at him confused. The warrior took her hand and put her narrow finger into the keyhole. He wanted her to try and pick the lock. Anna shrugged, and Khan-Tral nodded encouragement.

Instinctively, Anna drew a specific knife from her bandoleer. It was a stiletto. She stuck the narrow blade into the keyhole and twisted gently, feeling the inner workings and picturing them in her mind as if she had done it many times before. She wiggled the blade, and then there was an audible click and the door sagged. She turned to see Lamb giving her a look of surprise.

Khan-Tral cracked the door open and peered in the exposed direction. Then he opened the door a bit farther and looked furtively through the window. He shook his head, opened it all the way, and stepped through.

Anna stowed the stiletto and drew two larger blades from her collection. Lamb brandished the golden baton, though he did not know how it had done what it had done. Then they followed the warrior.

The dungeon was deserted. There were no signs of any activity, and all the cells they peeked into were empty. At the one end of the corridor, a formidable double-door stood partially open. A large chamber, clearly lit by flickering torches, stood beyond. The other end stretched endlessly into darkness.

Khan-Tral headed toward the double-doors as if he knew where he was going. He had drawn his enormous sword and held it at the ready with both hands. Anna made a mental note to stay back far enough to avoid his swing.

They crept toward the double-doors in silence, stepping carefully on the stone flags of the floor. Warm, dry air blew gently toward them from the room, which was unusual for an underground chamber, especially a large one.

When they reached the doors, the room was indeed very large. It was decorated in red with gold trim. Innumerable torches burned from sconces in the walls, but the room was primarily lit by the radiant glow from a pit in the center of the chamber.

At the opposite end of the room, beyond the pit, stood what looked like a column of translucent gold sitting on a marble pedestal. Inside the column was a young man who Anna knew was Brian Teplow.

Sitting on a raised throne next to the pedestal was a middle-aged man in red and gold robes with a crimson cape. A golden gorget hung from a chain around his neck. His evil face was crowned by a conical, red hat that matched his robes. He also held a crystal-tipped staff.

"You have finally arrived," the Red Wizard said with a malign smile.

Chapter 26

?

"YOUR TIME HAS COME, RED WIZARD!" Khan-Tral shouted, charging toward him with his sword poised for an overhead chop.

"Did you think it would be that easy?" Gho-Bazh taunted. With a wave of his staff, the perimeter of the chamber was lined with Pointees bearing jewel-tipped spears.

As in the New York Subway, the wizard's guards were slightly taller than Lamb and covered head to foot in coarse hair, though these wore their red and gold livery under armored, leather vests. Their feet were cloven and their heads were crowned with a pair of short, curved horns. Unlike the ones in New York, however these Pointees were not spectral, and had pronounced, goat-like snouts.

Khan-Tral was intercepted by four of the guards who appeared between him and his foe.

"Did you think that I didn't know of your tunnel? Or the catacombs beneath the palace?" He sneered. "Yes indeed, Nab," he said to Lamb, "why could they dig their way out? And where did the dirt go? You would think that a mountaintop fortress would be built on solid rock."

Anna was not surprised. This was the man from the cabinet in Rose's torture chamber. The Red Wizard from the dream she had had under the influence of the injection she received from Mickey Elder. Unlike everything else in this reality, the scene was different but the red-clothed man was still an adversary.

While the wizard and the swordsman exchanged words, she slowly made her way toward Khan-Tral, keeping him between her and the wizard.

"No so fast, assassin mine," Gho-Bazh said. Suddenly chains reappeared, connecting her wrist and ankle cuffs, and she fell forward onto her face. "You had your chance to regain my trust and kill the Queen of Brynner, but you failed." He looked at Lamb, who had not moved from the doorway, "So she sent you to kill me instead, with this bowless archer as a minder."

"WE CAME FOR DEB-ROH!" Khan-Tral said defiantly. The wizard was not amused.

"Must you always be so bombastic?" he said and waved his hand, and the warrior turned to stone. "You," he looked to Anna, "have another agenda, I think." He glanced at some of the guards along the wall, and two stepped forward, grabbed Anna under the arms, and dragged her before the throne. Lamb tried to come to her aid, but his path was blocked by crossed spears.

The Red Wizard stood and descended the pedestal to stand over Anna and take hold of her chin. "You wish to steal my companion from me." He turned her head toward the column.

It was Brian Teplow, dressed as described in his journals. He was alive and aware, but moved in extremely slow motions through the viscous golden fluid that filled the cylinder.

"Well," Gho-Bazh said, releasing her chin and walking behind her, "you cannot have him." He paced around the pit toward Lamb. "Deb-Roh is essential for the imprisonment of the Dark One. If he were to leave, or die, for that matter, this realm and everything in it would cease to be. The Dark One would again be free to tempt humanity and reap horror and despair on the real world."

"You know where we are?" Lamb asked in surprise.

"Of course," the wizard replied, turning on his heel to stand in the doctor's face. "This entire existence has been created from the mind of my good friend there. His abilities are so strong, especially when enhanced by the Siashutara serum, that he created everyone and everything here. Except us, of course."

"Why are you opposed to Utgarda?" Anna asked, straining against the grip of the Pointees, but hampered by her bonds.

"Utgarda," Gho-Bazh said conversationally, turning to walk back to Anna, "the Dark One, Satan, Loki, Coyote, Huehuecoyotl, Hanuman, Hermes, the Black Pharaoh. He has so many names across all of human history. But in all those innumerable forms, he has but one goal: to cruelly deceive and manipulate mankind and cause madness and destruction."

"He has tempted many over the course of millennia, causing the worst events in human history to pass. The Tower of Babel? Havoc caused by the Dark One. Pandora's box? Madness spread by Hermes. The Ten Plagues of Egypt. The Black Death.

"He offers wealth, or riches, or knowledge, or power," Gho-Bazh continued. "His resources are without end and his abilities indescribable. He has preyed on humanity for centuries, and we are helpless before him."

"And how did he tempt you?" Anna asked. "You are Meyer Kovacs, an eminent anthropologist." The wizard turned anxiously at the mention of the name. "Did the Dark One offer to bring back your wife?"

"No," he said. "I discovered commonalities among various cultures in the undeveloped world. Similar habits, patterns, symbols, stories. From the Incas to the Aborigines, the Mongols to the Maya, every culture had a version of the Dark One, and every culture had a tale of one who rose to greatness with his aid."

"I was under great pressure at that time," the wizard continued passionately. "I needed something extraordinary to make tenure. My peers were establishing a precise discipline and passing me by. Malinowski had embedded himself with a tribe of New Guinea natives and lived among them. Durkheim linked religion to the emotional security attained through communal living. Sapir was looking at the relationship between unique linguistic qualities and differences in cultural world views. I had to come up with something just as groundbreaking."

"And Utgarda helped you," Lamb said in accusation. Kovacs rounded on him.

"Yes. I was looking for the basis of magic in primitive societies. Laymen said that magic was just the catch-all explanation for the unknown, but I wanted to know how that practice and perception of magical rituals came about. I had read every tome and treatise on the topic. I visited tribes and villages all over the world. I focused on the undeveloped world as that was in vogue, and came up with common themes, but could not make the leap from belief to reality."

"And the Dark One offered the solution to you," Anna said, still on her knees, held down by the goat-men.

"No," the wizard said, turning to Anna. "He didn't tell me the solution, he gave it to me. He granted me the ability to do magic. Not illusion or deception, but the actual altering of reality." His tone changed and became more rational. "Of course, I knew that these powers had to be kept under control. I used them sparingly. I gave myself tenure. I made the program at Reister University important to the governors. I established myself as a notable persona in the field. Everything fit into place. Nicely. Cleanly. Without complications."

"But there was a price," Anna said knowingly. "There always is."

"Yes," the wizard said, his demeanor turning melancholic. "The dramatic changes I caused did not sit well with my wife. Each time I altered reality, she was altered along with it. At first, the changes were insignificant. A preference for orange over strawberry. Attacks of hay fever where she had previously not been affected."

"But as my station improved, her changes became more significant. When I received the Virchow Endowment, Maria started hearing everything. The settling of the house, creaks in the floorboards, insects in other rooms, the fluttering of birds outside. It grew steadily worse. I tried to use the power to help her, but I could not. I could only change things to improve myself."

"I used it one last time, to grant myself the latitude in my duties to take care of her, but that was the last straw. Her disability apparently had increased to the point where she could hear other people's thoughts. She refused to leave the house. And she declined steadily thereafter until she consumed an entire bottle of laudanum."

"I was consumed with guilt. I cloistered myself in my home and attempted to carry on, but I was a broken man. Over time, I became consumed with rage. I reached out with my powers. I did not care about consequences now. And I found

Brian Teplow. His psychic abilities were immense, but untapped. He was experimenting with experience-enhancing drugs that a vagrant he had encountered in the hospital was providing him." He gestured toward Khan-Tral.

"Brian had met Peter Gulden here in their collective imagination. In reality, Gulden was a drug-addled veteran of the Great War who was introduced to the Siashutara serum by Utgarda in France. Brian here created the story of their adventures together, and Gulden provided the Siashutara serum they used to return there for the next few years, where they gained a reputation."

"This is when I discovered Brian. His mind was able to create and sustain this world and everything in it. Using the powers Utgarda had given me, I entered this world and slowly established myself as an adversary worthy of heroes such as he had made of them. And when they came for me, I dominated Brian and kept him, imprisoned them, and initiated the rituals to trap the Dark One here."

"But the barbarian there broke them out of my dungeon and weakened the enchantment. The backlash sent them back to reality, along with fragments of this world. Teplow gained his spirit medium powers. He went home to his mother and fame and fortune. However, Peter Gulden returned to his helpless, aimless life."

"And the Dark One was once again free to prey on humanity. He sent his minions to stop me-"

"You mean the Junazhi," Anna said.

"Yes, the flying fungi. But I was too strong. They attempted to isolate my mind, and trapped me in an alien containment device. I resisted as best I could, but they eventually broke me. I was their prisoner, but they exposed me to their collective consciousness. I feigned catatonia, and learned the secrets of the universe.

"And then they brought Brian Teplow to me. They extracted his brain as well, and before they could assimilate him, I managed to escape the physical confines of my body and bring us both here. But Brian was not grateful. He attempted to flee, so I had to contain him and ensure that he maintained this realm indefinitely. So I trapped him in that stasis cylinder, where he exists at a fraction of real time, as much as time here can be considered real, so I can focus on binding the Dark One to this place and protecting the real world from him."

"But Utgarda needed Brian. It was a simple matter to lure Gulden back with more of the Siashutara serum. He extended some power to Gulden and charged him with finding him. When he was killed in the real world, Utgarda somehow managed to bring him here. But he was lost without his companion, and of no threat to me. Until now."

"And with Brian trapped here," Lamb interjected, "you have been capturing people to sacrifice for the spell to bind Utgarda?"

"That is correct," the wizard said with a sigh. "A necessary evil."

"But how is that any better than what Utgarda does in the real world?" Anna retorted. "Across human history, the trickster god tempts people into doing things that they know they should not. His victims are responsible for their own fate. You are stealing the lives of all those you sacrifice. You are responsible for their fates."

"But these are not real people," the wizard countered, kneeling next to Anna in front of Khan-Tral's statue. "These people are figments of Brian's imagination. They do not really exist. Their imitation sacrifice protects the people of the real world."

"They are as real here as you and me," Anna said. "You can touch them, you can see them, you can hurt them," she thought of Sobak, "and you can love them. They are as real as you believe them to be." She pondered that thought for a moment and drew a sly smile.

Chapter 27

?

They are as real as you believe them to be. Anna pondered that thought for a moment and drew a sly smile.

"They are as real as you believe them to be," she said again, aloud this time, concentrated, and the shackles, cuffs and all, disappeared. Gho-Bazh gaped in surprise.

She focused on Khan-Tral, and the swordsman reanimated. He had been in mid-strike when he was petrified, and upon coming back to life, continued the swing and chopped the Red Wizard in two with Nightbane. The shocked Gho-Bazh looked at Anna with surprise, and then his two halves parted in opposite directions.

Suddenly, the pillar containing Deb-Roh shattered and the golden fluid flooded out, washing over Anna, who was still on her hands and knees. There was a soothing sensation, and then the burning and sensitivity in her palms disappeared.

The Pointee guards were no longer unified. Some ran. Others dropped their spears. A few charged Anna and Khan-Tral. Some pointed their crystal spearheads toward the two. The two bloc   king Lamb were distracted by the attack on their master.

Taking advantage of this, Lamb clubbed one and then the other with the golden baton, and both were knocked down. He then pointed it at the rank of goat-men aiming at his friends and yelled. A burst of energy erupted from the baton and struck the line of Pointees.

Several of the guards dropped where they stood, their furry hides burning, but one fired a bolt that from his crystal that struck Khan-Tral in the back. The swordsman was in the middle of a swing, slicing through a circle of advancing foes just over Anna's head.

Brian Teplow stood disoriented in the midst of the confusion as several of the Pointees closed in on him. Anna threw a fusillade of knives, and then leapt forward and tackled him. Her blades expertly struck the oncoming guards, who fell or were knocked back by the impacts.

◆

"They've got Brian," O'Malley said with triumph. "Bring them back now." Bierce did not react at first. There was a brief flash of his attachment, and then nothing. O'Malley was suspicious. "What's going on?"

"The Junazhi sense that the realm known as Siashutara is becoming undone. Perhaps Brian Teplow is not in control of his senses, or has been disabled in some manner."

"What difference does that make? They did what you asked them to do. Kovacs is dead and they have Brian Teplow. Now tell them to bring them back here. Now!" Bierce's attachment flashed rapidly.

Suddenly, a Junazhi appeared next to Anna and Lamb's still forms. Something told O'Malley that they were in danger. He pointed the relic and fired. The alien disintegrated.

"Tell them to retrieve my friends now, or I will destroy everything here." To prove his point, he pointed the relic at a rack of brain canisters and destroyed it.

More Junazhi appeared, and O'Malley destroyed another. Their stalks and Bierce's attachment flashed furiously for several moments while the priest directed the device from one of the aliens to another. A Junazhi appeared next to the Kovacs cylinder, took hold of it, and then all the aliens disappeared.

"Kovacs' mind has been returned to his brain," Bierce said. **"They will retrieve your companions."**

O'Malley was inwardly relieved, but he suspected that something was still amiss.

"And bring them back here," he said, "alive and intact."

◆

"We need to get to the top of the tower," Lamb said, repeating a voice that he heard in his head.

"This way," Khan-Tral said, taking a staff from a fallen guard. As he turned, Anna noted the smoking, black wound in his back.

"You need medical attention," she said, gesturing urgently to Lamb.

"It is but a flesh wound," the warrior said with gritted teeth, and then pointed the staff at an ornate double-door and fired a beam at one of the guards emerging from it. The Pointee dropped, and the ones behind it stopped and lowered their spears.

"Come," the swordsman cried and ran toward a tapestry behind the throne. Anna took Brian's hand and dragged him toward the door.

Lamb yelled and another burst shot from the baton, felling the rest of the newcomers. He turned toward a group that had been approaching from behind, and they stopped in their tracks, their cloven hooves scoring the tiles. He backed away toward Anna and Khan-Tral.

The warrior tore off the tapestry to reveal a solid wall. Anna seemed to know where the discolored stone that opened the door was and pushed it. A section of the wall opened toward her.

Khan-Tral pointed his spear toward the oncoming guards as Lamb followed Anna through the door. Then he went through. Anna stepped on a certain stone in a circular stairway leading up. The door closed, and Khan-Tral rammed the staff into the crack at the bottom of the door, which was visible from that side, and jammed it in place.

Running up the steps two and three at a time, Anna stabbed a waiting Pointee guard at a landing and shoved it aside. Lamb followed with a smack in its forehead from the baton. The guard fell to the ground.

They continued up the steps. Lamb fired a blast, narrowly missing Anna, to roast several goat-men at the top of the stairway who were poised to fire. Khan-Tral ran past the other two. The wounded guards were in no condition to stop him from scanning a hallway that ran perpendicular to the stairway entrance. He fired his spear in one direction, and then stabbed an oncoming guard charging in from the other direction.

Anna, Brian, and Lamb caught up to him. Lamb fired the baton at a dozen Pointees advancing from the direction Khan-Tral had shot in, while the warrior drew Nightbane.

Anna threw another fusillade of blades toward the guards blocking the portal across the hallway, which led outside. She did not realize until she had thrown them that her bandoleer was emptied. All she had left were the two in her wrist sheaths.

◆

"Why can't the Junazhi just appear and bring them back?" O'Malley said anxiously.

"The Junazhi cannot materialize in the realm of Brian Teplow's imagination. They must use an access point that he has provided. They are en route to retrieve your friends."

◆

Anna, Brian, Lamb, and Khan-Tral crossed an open courtyard. Brian was not athletic, and Anna and Lamb held him by the arms to keep him moving. The Pointee guards there were in a state of confusion, running in all directions, some colliding with others. Several were fighting. Some used their spears, while others just butted their horned heads. The human trio avoided confrontation, but Lamb blasted the path ahead of them to keep it clear. They ran toward the entrance of the central tower.

Suddenly, fresh bolts started striking all around them. Goat-man guards on the walls were firing their spears into the courtyard, striking their peers in an attempt to hit the fleeing trio. They took cover behind a stone well. Lamb blasted the guards on the wall who could still see them as the well was rapidly demolished by the barrage from the walls.

Then they heard screeching, and shadows fell across the keep as scores of the flying Draunskur dove in and attacked the guards on the walls. The defenders in the courtyard took cover and started firing at the aerial threat.

Khan-Tral threw the gasping Brian over his shoulder and sprinted with Anna and Lamb for the open door to the tower.

Once inside, they kept moving, leaping up the circular stairway and ignoring whatever might be inside the tower. They guards they encountered were firing their spears through the open windows. Anna and Lamb ran past, but Khan-Tral paused long enough to push the guards out.

When they reached the trapdoor to the roof of the tower, Anna and Lamb stopped to catch their breath and waited for Khan-Tral to catch up. After a moment, they started to worry, but Brian Teplow stumbled up the steps, breathing heavily.

"Where is Khan-Tral?" Anna asked.

"He's- holding them off," Teplow wheezed out. Lamb pulled Brian's arm over his shoulder and lifted him to his feet.

Anna climbed the short ladder, slid the bolts from the trapdoor, and flung it open. The orange-red sky was turning cloudy and a malevolent purple. Blue bolts of lightning flashed among the clouds.

She climbed onto the roof and then lowered a hand to help pull Brian up. Lamb followed and they sat against the crenellations.

"We should close the hatch," Lamb said.

"What about Khan-Tral?" Anna asked.

"He's not coming," Brian said in resignation. "He holds them off so we can escape. That's how I would have written the story."

Anna wanted to protest, but she knew the swordsman would not be coming with them. That was not part of the deal with Junazhi.

Lamb closed the hatch. There were no bolts on this side.

"What happens now?" Anna asked.

"We wait, I guess," Lamb replied.

◆

All around, the flyers dove and slashed at the goat-men. From their vantage, Anna could see the former shot out of the sky by the blasts, and the latter drawn up and dropped from high above them

The blue-tinged lightning grew closer and more frequent. She wondered if being on the top of a tower in a lightning storm was a good idea. Perhaps they should have waited inside.

Suddenly, there was a distant buzzing sound. As it grew closer, that familiar feeling of dread appeared and increased. She peered over the wall of the tower and saw three long, gnarled, bulbous bodies flying toward them. As they became more distinct, the numerous stalks on their heads and the five pairs of legs identified them as Junazhi.

"Our ride is here," Anna said with an ironic smile. She helped the reluctant Brian to his feet. He turned pale when he saw them.

"I'm not going anywhere with *them*," he said.

"Everything will be fine," Anna said calmly. "We have made an arrangement with them. We traded Kovacs for you, and we will be taking you home to your mother as soon as we get back."

Teplow glanced from Anna to Lamb to the approaching Junazhi. He sighed loudly, gave a tentative smile, and said, "Perhaps flying through space with my brain is a can won't be so bad."

The Junazhi reached the top of the tower, and in a single, fluid motion, each one grabbed a member of the trio under the arms gently but firmly with their six legs and flew off. Anna felt a pinch as a finger from the alien's front claws pierced into each of her ears, then her vision was fixed downward and she was in a state of complete relaxation and comfort.

They went up the slopes and beyond the snow-capped Groaning Slopes of Woe into the purple-pink sky high above the Endless Barrens of None. The plain turned into frozen tundra, and at the first sign of snow, the flight turned upward into the night sky and then everything went black.

Chapter 28

July 17, 1929

O'Malley relaxed slightly when he saw Anna, Lamb, and Brian Teplow collected from the tower by the Junazhi. They appeared to fly off rapidly into space, and then the image went blank.

"What happened?" he said anxiously. They were so close.

"Doctor Lamb has fallen unconscious. Perhaps from lack of oxygen."

"The Junazhi know that they need oxygen to breathe, right?"

"Of course they do. But at that altitude, the air must be quite thin."

"I suppose that makes sense," O'Malley conceded, but then added, "but I expect them to be here, alive and intact, any time now."

"I don't know how long a journey between dimensions takes, but the Junazhi have no concept of psychological manipulation. They will not delay to prolong your distress."

Suddenly, the inert forms of Anna and the doctor faded away. O'Malley leapt to where they had been, but only the blankets remained. He pointed the relic at another shelf.

"Have the Junazhi betrayed them?" he said through gritted teeth. "I want to know what happened. Now!"

Bierce's attachment flashed for an extended period. A Junazhi appeared and O'Malley saw its stalks flash in conversation with the device.

"The Junazhi have not deceived you. There can only be one incarnation of a being in a given dimension. That is why they could not just appear in the other realm. They exist simultaneously across all dimensions and so could not duplicate themselves there."

"So what happened to Harry and Anna?"

"The disappearance of their physical forms means that they have already passed into this dimension. They will return soon."

◆

The wait seemed endless. O'Malley was tempted to destroy more of the racks, but realized that that would not actually accomplish anything. Bierce did not seem to know any more than he did.

Eventually, his stress overcame him, because he was awakened by a gentle touch on the cheek. He opened his eyes and Anna smiled down at him. She wore the leather garments he had seen on the screen, and had a pair of knives strapped to her forearms.

"That's a new look for you," he said groggily with a smile. Anna pulled him to his feet for a hug.

"Good to see that our ordeal was not too taxing on you," Lamb said, noting the priest's weariness, but also the china tea set and a plate bearing pastry crumbs on the table next to the Bierce device.

"I was afraid you would not return!" O'Malley replied earnestly, hurriedly releasing Anna. "I destroyed several of those creatures and the rack that used to be over there!" He indicated the empty space on the far end of the side wall.

"Relax, Sean," Lamb said with a smile, clapping the Father on the back. "I was just toying with you." Lamb embraced him. "I'm glad to see that you are well."

"This is Brian Teplow," Anna said, introducing the short, sandy-haired, young man. "Brian, this is Father Sean O'Malley, who has been working with us to find you."

"Um," Teplow seemed disoriented, "nice to meet you, Father?" O'Malley guided him to the chair he had been sitting in and poured a cup of tea.

"Drink this," the priest said, handing Teplow the cup.

"It needs sugar," Brian said after he took a sip. O'Malley gave him a spoon and the sugar bowl. "So what made you want to come and look for me?"

"We can talk about that on our way back to the city," Anna said.

Suddenly, half a dozen Junazhi appeared. Their head stalks flashed in strobing patterns as if synchronized.

"**The Junazhi cannot allow you to leave,**" the Bierce device said. "**The agreement was for you to make contact with Mr. Teplow in exchange for restoring Kovacs' mind to his brain. The terms of that agreement have been successfully completed.**"

"They said nothing of keeping us here," Anna snapped. "We did as they asked, and now we are leaving. By their leave or not!"

The aliens approached to surround the group. O'Malley pointed the relic and disintegrated one of them.

Unnoticed by anyone, Lamb had pulled the golden baton from his quiver while the others were talking with Teplow. Now he pointed it toward the bulk of the approaching Junazhi, and his blast incinerated four of them.

Three more appeared, spaced out to be prevent Lamb from hitting more than one of them.

O'Malley turned the relic on the racks of brain cylinders and started shooting them. At the same time, Anna dove onto Brian, pushing the chair over backward and depositing them on the floor behind it.

One by one, the priest disintegrated the shelves and their contents while Lamb fired and destroyed the aliens. Finally, new Junazhi stopped appearing.

The basement chamber smelled of burnt meat, dust, and something indescribable and unpleasant. Somewhere along the way, Billy had been caught in the crossfire, and lay in a barely recognizable charred hulk on the floor.

"It is time to go," Anna said. She glanced around at the carnage, and then led Brian out the door and up the stairs. Lamb followed, still keeping the baton at the ready.

O'Malley took a moment to collect his thoughts. He turned back to the Bierce device.

"What would you like me to do?" he asked the cylinder.

"**This existence has its benefits**," the staccato monotone said, "**Believe it or not, I am content with my current state. As for the others, I cannot say. For all the minds that you destroyed, I see no reason to leave those on the shelves. Without any of the sensory attachments, they have no interaction with the world around them.**"

O'Malley nodded, took a moment to collect their possessions, and then disintegrated the final rack of brain cylinders.

"Farewell, Mr. Bierce.

Chapter 29

August 2, 1929

"I know you are there," Anna said. She was reclining in a chaise lounge on the patio of Dr. Feldman's house outside Westerberg. She wore a light, yellow sun dress with a floral pattern.

The intruder continued to approach, attempting to be sneaky. In a flash, Anna threw a pen, a teaspoon, and a butter knife at him. Then she opened her eyes to see Sean O'Malley grinning with an impressed expression, rubbing his forehead where the projectiles had hit him.

"You seem to have retained the abilities Brian ascribed to you in Siashutara," the Father said, taking a seat beside her in a neighboring chair.

"So it would appear," she said introspectively. In the two weeks since they had returned Brian Teplow to his mother in

Brooklyn, Anna and Lamb had been staying at Feldman's estate. O'Malley had been busy pursuing church business.

Unlike the priest, the trustees had not yet made their determination regarding Anna and Lamb's positions with the Reister University, even though the Longborough affair was now old news.

◆

Following a long hike along the path next to the telephone lines, Anna, Lamb, O'Malley, and Teplow arrived at a road. There, they hitched a ride back to Chatham with a farmer. O'Malley explained his companions' odd attire by saying that they were lost circus performers. From there, O'Malley purchased train tickets for them and they returned to the city.

On the train, Anna told Brian about the request Jason Longborough had asked them to perform, including all the supernatural details. Brian listened to the story with rapt interest.

"Mr. Longborough's wife told us that he had been extremely stressed for some time," Anna said, "but that he came to see you in the city, and whatever transpired between you seemed to calm him."

"She said he was a changed man," O'Malley added.

"Would you mind telling us about that conversation?" Lamb asked.

"I think I owe it to you," Brian said. "It's the least I can do." He took a deep breath and collected his thoughts.

"Jason came to see me in late April or early May. He had the gold box you spoke of with him." Teplow thought for a moment. "He told me that he and some college friends had dabbled in the occult when he was younger, and that they had released something evil into the world." Brian shuddered.

"He asked me to see what I could get from the box. When I took hold of it, I believe I told him that all his preparations were complete and the pieces were in place. Or something to that effect."

"What did you see?" Anna asked.

"I saw from Utgarda's perspective, the giant version, winged figures flying across the horizon over the Endless Plains of None. I could tell that they were the solution to his worries." He grew serious.

"What else?" O'Malley said with anticipation.

"I saw that I would go through an unpleasant trial, but that I would come through. I didn't tell Longborough that. The look of relief on the old man's face was powerful."

"That's all?" Lamb said with surprise and indignation, and then. "I'm sorry."

"That was it," Teplow said with a nod. "We only met for half an hour or so."

◆

Anna and O'Malley joined Feldman and Lamb on a wide expanse of lawn. Various targets had been set up at different distances, and Lamb had been shooting at them with a number of weapons, some of which the librarian had acquired on loan from museums or collectors he knew.

"Your abilities are astounding," Feldman said, looking through a pair of binoculars at a paper bullseye swinging in the light breeze from a tree perhaps 300 yards away. "Even with a moving target, you hit it square in the center."

Lamb shrugged when he saw the two approaching and set the crossbow down on a table next to a variety of bows, spears, a blowgun, and other more-exotic devices.

"What have you learned?" Anna asked.

"I'm useless throwing things-" Lamb started to say.

"By useless," Feldman interrupted, "he means that he does not always hit the target, but there isn't a baseball team that wouldn't want Dr. Lamb here."

"I'm also pretty good at golf," Lamb added with grin, "but I was no sap before this adventure."

"These skills are all well and good," O'Malley said, "but I don't expect that you will have much use for them in academia."

"About that," Feldman said awkwardly. "The trustees have not met to deliberate your case yet. Apparently several are unavailable until September, so you are going to be in limbo for a while longer. You're both welcome to stay here as long as you like, but eventually you will need to get back to your own lives-" He left the sentence hanging.

"I have been considering my options," Anna said. "This experience has renewed my interest in field work. My position with Reister University was only temporary until Dr. McMahon returns from Australia anyway. What about you?" She turned to Lamb.

"Well," he said, "It appears that I could give up medicine for a career as a sharpshooter or ball player." He thought for a moment and a smile bloomed, "I could get a pilot's license! Flyboys need good eyesight, and mine is amazing now!"

"Your gifts would also enable you to be an excellent surgeon," O'Malley said. "As for me, the Church has continued my assignment here for the time being."

"There is another option," Feldman said. The three turned to him with suspicion. "I told you that I had retained Mr. Cophen to investigate matters such as the Longborough affair. The trust fund provided financing for such activities."

"At the recommendation of a financial advisor who is aware of the fund and its purpose, we established the Longborough Foundation for Ethnographic Research. Under the guise of an academic institution, the Foundation can actively address the 'unexplainable events' that the fund was initially established to deal with, and I would like you three to take over for Mr. Cophen."

"So you're suggesting that we come to work for this Longborough Foundation as occult investigators," Lamb said in a tone that was both surprised and intrigued.

"That is correct," Feldman replied. "The Foundation would provide you with an appropriate salary and accommodations, as well as acquire whatever resources and equipment you might need."

"How often do these kind of events occur?" Anna asked.

"More often that you would think," O'Malley said. He considered for a moment, and then said, "I am part of a holy order dedicated to fighting these supernatural phenomena. The Order of Saint Dionysius the Aeropagite, who is the patron saint of protection from the devil, by the way, has been fighting this battle for centuries. Vatican politics are threatening the activities of the Order. This foundation would be able to carry on that holy work, perhaps even with the Church's blessing and support."

"Even so," Lamb interjected, "you can't predict when the supernatural will impose itself on the real world. How will we know when we are needed? And what will be do in the meantime?"

"I have a network of like-minded associates throughout the world," Feldman said, "who are on the lookout for unexplainable phenomena. They will report such things to me."

"And the Church has the greatest reach on the planet," O'Malley added. "Reports of incursions by the devil and his minions are received by the Order every day. They could channel those reports to us as well."

"You seem to already know about all this," Anna said. "How is that?"

"I mentioned the situation in Rome to Dr. Feldman in passing. I contacted him when I arrived in New York and you failed to meet my boat," O'Malley said.

"I was already aware of the Order," Feldman continued, "and made some discrete inquiries of my own. Since your return, Father O'Malley has been acting as an official go-between with Vatican representatives, whom he has been meeting with in Boston."

"So you've been keeping this from us," Lamb said. "When did you intend to tell Anna and I about your plans?"

"I was waiting to hear from Father O'Malley," Feldman replied. "I trust all went well."

"Archbishop Szamosközy was not able to commit to funding," O'Malley replied, "but agreed that channeling activities to the Foundation, and therefore removing them from direct Vatican involvement, would ensure that the goals of the Order continued to be pursued."

"This sounds like a setup," Lamb said.

"I have been thinking about this direction for some time," Feldman said. "With the appearance of the three of you, and with the abilities you now possess, it seems like the time to act is now. What do you say?"

ABOUT THE AUTHOR

Joab Stieglitz was born and raised in Warren, New Jersey. He is an Application Consultant for a software company. He has also worked as a software trainer, a network engineer, a project manager, and a technical writer over his 30-year career. He lives in Alexandria, Virginia.

Joab is an avid tabletop RPG player and game master of horror, espionage, fantasy, and science fiction genres, including Savage Worlds (Mars, Deadlands, Agents of Oblivion, Apocalypse Prevention Inc, Herald: Tesla and Lovecraft, Thrilling Tales, and others), Call of Cthulhu, Lamentations of the Flame Princess, Pugmire, and Pathfinder.

Joab channeled his role-playing experiences in the Utgarda Series, which are pulp adventure novels with Lovecraftian influences set in the 1920's.

You can follow Joab on Twitter @JoabStieglitz, on Facebook, and on his blog: joabstieglitz.com.

JOAB STIEGLITZ

THE OLD MAN'S REQUEST

BOOK ONE OF THE UTGARDA SERIES

The Old Man's Request
Book One of the Utgarda Series

Fifty years ago, a group of college friends dabbled in the occult and released a malign presence on the world. Now, on his deathbed, the last of the students, now a trustee of Reister University enlists the aid of three newcomers to banish the thing they summoned.

Russian anthropologist Anna Rykov, doctor Harry Lamb, and Father Sean O'Malley are all indebted the ailing trustee for their positions. Together, they pursue the knowledge and resources needed to perform the ritual.
Hampered by the old man's greedy son, the wizened director of the university library, and a private investigator with a troubled past, can they perform the ritual and banish the entity?

The Old Man's Request is a pulp adventure set in the 1920s, and the first book in the Utgarda Series.

Available in paperback and ebook formats, and as an Audible audiobook

THE
MISSING
MEDIUM
BOOK TWO OF THE UTGARDA SERIES
JOAB STIEGLITZ

The Missing Medium
Book Two of the Utgarda Series

While Father Sean O'Malley is summoned to Rome to discuss the "Longborough Affair" with his superiors, Russian anthropologist Anna Rykov and Doctor Harold Lamb travel to New York City where they encounter merchants, mobsters and madmen in pursuit of the spirit medium who advised their mentor shortly before the start of the whole adventure.

The Missing Medium is a pulp adventure set in the 1920s, and the second book in the Utgarda Series.

Available in paperback and ebook formats, and as an Audible audiobook

THE HUNTER
IN THE
SHADOWS
BOOK ONE OF THE THULE TRILOGY
JOAB STIEGLITZ

The Hunter in the Shadows
Book One of the Thule Trilogy

After dreaming that her alter-dimensional sister Sobak was in danger, Anna Rykov is sent to Depression era Boston to find and kill the shape shifting alien who has captured her, and whose plans could bring about the extinction of all life on Earth

Anna is assisted by Cletus the hound and a homeless World War I veteran with skeletons in his own closet. However, Anna's inquiries catch the attention of J. Edgar Hoover, whose motives in this case are unknown.

The Hunter in the Shadows is a pulp adventure set in the 1930s, is the first book in the Thule Trilogy, and the fourth book in the Utgarda Series.

Available in paperback and ebook formats, and as an Audible audiobook